FOUND *you*

DAHLIA DONOVAN

HOT TREE PUBLISHING

For information, contact the publisher, Hot Tree Publishing.

www.hottreepublishing.com

Editing: Hot Tree Editing

Designer: BookSmith Design

Ebook ISBN-13: 978-1-925448-60-3

Paperback ISBN-13: 978-1-925448-61-0

To the judged and brokenhearted—never give up on finding love.

PROLOGUE
DUSK

September

In the aftermath of yet another hurricane, his entire world had been destroyed. His vet clinic with the apartment over it? Completely trashed. His Jeep Wrangler? Wrapped around one of the trees across the street which wasn't the end of the world since he used his bicycle more. His parents' bar hadn't been spared either and had significant damage from the winds and storm surge.

His insurance agent told him to consider it the cost of doing business in Key West. She'd also explained how his policy didn't cover all of the damage. He would barely get 30 percent of the cost to rebuild his life's work.

"Maybe you should consider moving further north?"

Move?

Move.

Every year during hurricane season, tourists, friends, and extended family always seemed to take great pleasure in questioning his sanity for living in the Keys all year. None of them understood. He thrived in the Florida Keys in a way he couldn't anywhere else.

His hippie parents had moved to Key West in the seventies to start up their little bar. The dingy Barefoot Saloon served mostly local fishermen; tourists found it too *colorful* for their tastes. He'd grown up in that free-spirited atmosphere, homeschooled by his mother who let him do his schoolwork in a corner booth while she served drinks and vegetarian fare.

Education had been the only thing to draw him away from home. He had left to study Animal Science at the University of Florida. Gainesville had seemed almost a different world to him at eighteen.

Animal Science had led him, after four years, to the College of Veterinary Medicine. He had eventually graduated and interned with a clinic in Jacksonville for a further two years. Only then had he moved back to Key West to start his own practice.

For two years, he had run the Dusk Til Dawn Animal Hospital out of a converted beach cottage on White Street a few blocks away from his parents' bar. It had been his pride and joy. He loved working with the wide variety of critters brought into his office.

And then fuck-a-doodle-do, a hurricane had to come and spit in his eyes.

"Dusk Keller."

He glanced over his shoulder from where he'd been tugging the tree branches out of the middle of what had been the front desk and the waiting area of his clinic. "Jesse."

Jesse had lived in Key West for over twenty years. He'd arrived on Dusk's seventh birthday, having drifted ashore in a banged up life raft. He claimed to have no memory of where or when his boat had sunk or what his last name was. "Want a hand?"

"Mom cut you off again?" Dusk had to laugh at the contrite expression on the old man's face. She cut Jesse off at least once a week when he'd annoyed the other regulars too much. "I could use a second set of hands."

His helper turned out to be *not* quite so useful. Jesse spent more time bemoaning spots on his shoulder, that he thought might be shingles, and less actually lifting anything heavier than a leaf. Dusk leaned against a ruined section of wall to survey what felt like an insurmountable amount of work.

"Here, look."

"Jesse, I don't want to look at your damn shingles." Dusk could never get the man to understand he worked on animals—not the two-legged variety. "I don't want to sniff them or touch them."

"Useless doctor."

"Vet."

"Same shit."

"No, it really, really isn't." Dusk grimaced when Jesse lifted his shirt. "Don't mind me while I lose my lunch."

"Useless."

"Dusk, honey, are you there?"

With a grateful sigh of relief, Dusk hopped over the growing pile of rubble to join his mom on the side-walk. She handed him a paper sack and a large bottle of water. Her gaze hardened when she spotted Jesse.

"I'll be going." Jesse made a quick escape.

Dusk snickered until his mom smacked him on the arm. Even at twenty-seven, his mom treated him as if he were a young teenager. "How's Pops?"

"Arguing with the contractor."

Unlike him, his parents had been wise enough to opt for all possible additions to their insurance policy.

The Barefoot Saloon would be completely restored to its dubious former glory within weeks. They still managed to serve beers on the veranda, and maybe the inspectors wouldn't like it, but no one ever told them.

"We could help, honey."

Dusk shook his head at her. "No, mom, I told you."

They had paid for his education and helped him start the clinic in the first place. He refused to take another dime from them. He could manage it by himself—somehow.

Even if he had to resort to walking dogs and making home visits.

1

———

KENT

November

As a man voted most likely to be president, Kent thought his fall from grace painfully sudden. Divorced. Broke. He had become estranged from family and friends, living in a rundown shack in Key West. It was a far cry from the wealthy, successful real estate mogul who had built a business flipping houses with his handsome husband in the rich suburbs of Denver.

Finding his twenty-year-old carpenter in bed with his husband, Spencer, had soured their relationship of over twenty years. The separation had been an inevitable conclusion. They might've been the second same-sex marriage in Colorado's history, but they'd been the first divorce.

Together for twenty years plus, married for barely long enough to have a second anniversary. Pathetic. I'm in my forties. Life shouldn't be falling apart now.

The affair had been the last drop in a dangerously overfilled cup. Spencer had been accusing him of being too focused on work for years. *Funny.* Kent found it ironic given how he since had nothing, and his ex-husband had taken everything they had built together.

No damn prenup.

He hadn't seen the point of dragging things out in court. He told his attorney to give it all to Spencer. Everything but the cottage in Key West that he had wanted to keep.

His sister constantly reminded him that he could turn the place in Florida into something more. He didn't have the heart to tell her the cottage was a broken-down, hurricane-damaged ruin. It wasn't fit for much.

Just like me. Oh, there they are. Every. Damn. Morning. Woof. Woof. Woof. Bawk. Bawk. Bawk. Every Damn. Morning.

Key West might have the reputation of paradise on

earth, yet it seemed more paradise lost than anything. It was hotter than his old home in Castle Rock, Colorado. Never mind the crazed wildlife, both of the human and non-human variety that cavorted freely around the streets and beaches.

Like clockwork for the last four days, his sleep had been interrupted between five and seven in the morning. A local dog walker's path took him right by the beach cottage with a group of mangy mutts. *Oh.* He also had the pleasure of dealing with chickens wandering by at irregular hours, clucking and scratching.

Had he moved to a farm or the beach?

Kent sat on the battered steps to his cottage with lukewarm coffee, searching for the subject of his ire and easily spotting him traipsing up the sand. "Hey."

Mr. Dog Walker grinned and waved enthusiastically. "Morning. I'm Dusk Keller. I saw you move in a few days ago. You here for Thanksgiving or more permanently?"

Dusk? Who the hell names their kid Dusk?

And what grown man doesn't immediately change his name when he's of age?

"Kent Casado. It's a semipermanent move. Dusk? Did your parents lose a bet or something?" He couldn't help the question, not when faced with someone obviously in their midtwenties having such a ridiculous name. "Was drinking involved?"

"Drinking? No. I'm sure pot and mushrooms might've affected their decision-making skills." Dusk hadn't stopped grinning. "How do you like it here so far?"

"The mornings are as enjoyable as having a tooth pulled." Kent glared bitterly at his empty cup of coffee. "Do you have to walk the damn dogs every morning?"

"I do." He shifted a little further down the beach when the animals tugged on the leashes in his hand. "See you tomorrow."

Wonderful.

While Dusk drifted away from him, Kent found himself drawn to inspecting the man. He had longish dirty-blond hair, wavy, and out-of-control; it matched the scruff on his face which was barely more than a five o'clock shadow. He had tanned skin likely from days spent under the heat of the Florida sun, which only served to make his incredible blue eyes stand out.

Those eyes glanced back toward him as if sensing his perusal. Dusk winked at him and waved cheerily. It only worked to make the blue even brighter.

Kent could easily spot at least three tattoos on the

dog walker with his beach attire of khaki shorts and a tank top. He had an island and ocean scene on his left arm while his right had several symbols on it that looked almost like doctor symbols, but might've been for a vet instead. The edges of some sort of map peeked out from under his shirt in the back.

A few more steps sent Dusk out of his view. It left Kent with one lasting impression—the man did have a nice ass. He might put up with the barking dogs for a closer look at it each morning. Not the chickens, however. Maybe he could write to Popeye's to offer them up. The locals might not be too thrilled with him, but he might get to sleep in a little.

Stretching his legs out until his feet dug into the sand, Kent relaxed against the steps with his eyes closed against the sun. Florida had certainly not done anything for his productivity. His type-A need to accomplish tasks had taken a nosedive over the last few weeks.

His sister wrote him ten-page letters about how she thought he might be depressed.

"You miss Spencer," she'd write amongst a multitude of other comments on his "delicate emotional state—post divorce."

Miss Spencer? He didn't.

Okay.

He did—a little.

Get off your ass, old man. The house isn't going to build itself.

Might be nice if it would.

2

DUSK

DUSK RETURNED THE DOGS TO THE HOTEL WHERE THEIR various owners stayed. He'd known the manager for years, and she was more than thrilled to throw work his way to help him save up for rebuilding the clinic. Some days he had twenty dogs to walk, others none at all.

He grabbed his favorite pumpernickel bagel from Goldman's on Roosevelt with the green tea they stocked especially for him. *Breakfast of champions.* It was early enough that the few tourists there were hadn't ventured out of their rooms yet.

November generally signaled the end of hurricane season. It might rain periodically, but more often than not, the weather turned beautiful. He strolled down to the beach, without four-legged friends this time, to enjoy his bagel.

For several months, Dusk had split his time between clearing out the clinic, walking dogs, and home visits with his clients. He figured the debris and damaged parts would be completely removed by mid-December. *Maybe.* He worried there wouldn't be enough cash to pay the contractors to rebuild.

His thoughts had been entirely consumed with trying to think of ways to earn the money. His parents had offered to help, again. He couldn't accept it, though, wanting to stand on his own two feet.

Jenna, an old college friend, had suggested a GoFundMe campaign. Dusk had never been a fan of the Internet, so she had offered to create it for him and handle it.

GoFundMe would be way too much like charity. Other people in the Keys were far more deserving of that sort of help. He told her to work her magic for the locals who couldn't afford to rebuild their homes after the destructive storm.

He had a home.

Everything else will take care of itself.

Taking in slow, deep breaths, Dusk decided to enjoy the briny ocean breeze unsullied by all the scents that came with crowded beaches. Mornings had a purity to them. He communed with the sound of the waves on the sand, the fizzing of the foam spreading along the shore. It buoyed his spirit.

If Dusk had a religion, his chapel would be the beach. Hymns would be sung to the rhythm of the waves. Who needed incense when the salt in the air filled his nostrils? Lines of scripture would be written in the sand, and in fact, might do more for souls than the judgmental nonsense some claimed to be God's word.

Finishing up his bagel, he crumpled up the paper and shoved it into his pocket to throw in the trash later. His fingers plucked up a nearby shell and traced the sharp ridges on the outside of it absently. He wondered if Kent Casado, the grumpy man from the beach, would pay him to help around the cottage. Couldn't hurt to ask, right?

He considered the odds of Mr. Grumpy biting his head off—high. *Maybe a bagel will improve his mood?* Dusk had inherited a spirit of never giving up from his mom. His dad had gifted him with a love of walking barefoot and playing his guitar on street corners; they'd often sung and played together before Pops' eyes started to fail.

His heart sank a little at the thought of Pops' last visit to the doctor. The stubborn old man had refused to go for years; it had taken the hurricane to change his mind. Unable to see clearly, his dad had gotten lost while attempting to turn on the generator when they lost power.

Dusk and Jesse had searched in the middle of the worst of the storm for him. He had thought for heartbreaking moments that his beloved Pops had died. It had been the kick in the behind required to get both of his parents to take their health seriously.

Burying the shell in the sand, Dusk got to his feet. He wouldn't accomplish anything sitting and enjoying the music of the ocean. The universe hadn't given him that sort of life.

"Dr. Dusky."

Dusk covered his face with his hands and groaned. Why had he decided to return to his hometown after university? Some people would forever see him as the towheaded, scrawny kid who delivered papers, cupcakes, and beers. "Now, Miss Alice, what are you doing up so early?"

She waved her diamond-ring-covered fingers at him. "My Fluffy broke a nail. Will you check on her later?"

"Yes, ma'am."

The Fluffy in question happened to be an overweight Himalayan cat that had some sort of ailment at least once a week. Miss Alice had the distinction of being the only surviving daughter of an old money family from South Carolina. She owned a large home and lived in it with her butler and her cat.

She tended to pay at least three times the amount on her bills, and always pinched his butt. *Always.* In her eighties, she had more energy than he did. He politely declined all invitations to visit her bedroom.

His attempts at dissuading her from making the request failed consistently. She didn't seem to care that he was gay. "It's all right, Dusky darling. I'm so old it all looks the same."

No, no it doesn't.

He had nightmares about it. His mom laughed every time he asked her to talk with Miss Alice about her propositioning. *Not helpful.* She still giggled whenever the older woman came into the bar for her afternoon drink.

"Well, darling?"

Dusk shook his head to focus on the eighty-two-year-old in front of him. "I'll be sure to swing by this afternoon."

"And stay for dinner?"

"You're a sweetheart, Miss Alice, but I'm eating with my folks this evening," he lied, with a pleasant smile on his face, and he hoped to hell she didn't ask his mom, who would take great joy in suggesting he eat with the lonely senior. "You have a good morning."

With highly uncomfortable visuals dancing uninvited in his mind, Dusk went quickly in the opposite direction of the grand dame of Key West. He deftly avoided her pinching fingers. He couldn't help the shudder that flowed through his entire body. He would visit Mr. Grumpy in the morning.

Think about the money to build the clinic. Don't think about naked old people. Oh. Eww.

3

———

KENT

THE CHICKENS AND DOGS HADN'T WOKEN HIM UP FOR once. It had been a knock on the door with a special delivery from his attorneys in Denver. He tossed the envelope to the side and stared morosely at the toaster, waiting somewhat patiently for his frozen waffles. The finalized divorce papers had also included a note from his sister about calling his mother.

Spencer had been the chef. If it couldn't be microwaved, Kent had no idea what to do with it. For months, it had frustrated him how thoughts always drifted back to his previous life.

He had met his ex-husband in college when they'd both been in their early twenties. Now in his forties, it seemed so long ago. They'd been young, so young, and full of hopes and dreams for their future together.

They'd built a construction business. The market crash had initially brought them closer as a couple, or so he thought.

His decision to throw himself into working hard to maintain their lifestyle had clearly come at the cost of their relationship. He'd wrongly assumed Spencer understood. It had only taken arriving home early to discover how incredibly mistaken he'd been.

Finding his husband in bed with a man twenty years younger had been a punch to the gut. Kent hadn't been so angry since his uncle called him a failure for his "queer tendencies." He hadn't been to a family dinner since.

He hadn't been to a family *anything*.

The move to Key West provided a much-needed separation from his family. They hadn't wasted any time in mocking him over the breakup of his marriage. *Told you so.* His mother and her side of the family had never been supportive of anything that hinted at same-sex.

Raised by a single mother, Kent had often dreamed as a child that his father would come find him. He knew nothing about the man. He only had the man's last name and his eyes, both inherited.

His mother's family had refused to allow him to have their surname. The Edwards of Colorado came from a long line of Baptist ministers. His grandfather was a pastor; his grandfather's father was a pastor, and so on. The family practically bled scripture verses, and he hadn't fit in with them at all.

Ramon Casado had been his dad. He had the man's name, genetics, eyes, and height, since he'd always stood head and shoulders above the Edwardses. Maybe one day he would search for his father. The man would likely be in his sixties, wasn't too late yet.

Maybe one day.

His sister had been far luckier. She was the child of his mother and step-father, a man Grandpa Edwards had approved of completely. She also looked the spitting image of their mother, long black hair, rich umber skin, and startling hazel eyes.

Not mixed blood, like me.

Setting aside the disturbing memories from both the distant and recent past, Kent perused the list that he had jotted down the previous night. The roof had already been repaired. It had been the first and most critical of his projects; today he'd continue working on the exterior.

The interior could be saved for days when the rain made being outside a misery. Shutters had to be replaced along with getting rid of the peeling paint. He'd fix the one broken section of the outer wall and hopefully, shore up the busted stairs at the rear of the cottage if the lumber arrived on time.

A big if.

One of his old friends from college who owned a construction business in Miami had promised to send a truck out with supplies. Kent had offered to cover the cost but was told to consider it a debt paid in full.

Just as Kent attempted to focus on the list again, a knock on the door pulled him away. He found the shaggy dog-walker standing cheerfully with two paper cups and a brown sack, no dogs in sight. What did the idiot want now?

"Bagel?" Dusk shook the bag before barging forward past a shell-shocked Kent into the cottage. "Hope you take your coffee black. You look like you would. I bet you're a black coffee and an everything bagel type of man, all button-up shirts and clean shaves."

"Any other insights you'd like to share?"

Dusk's blue eyes twinkled mischievously at him. "You're grumpy, like an old rooster who can't crow anymore. You work too hard and think too much. You've been here how long, but never once actually enjoyed the beach."

"Did you by chance earn a psychology degree while walking dogs?"

"I'm a vet, not a shrink." Dusk waved the bag for the second time, giving it a third shake. "Want the bagel or not?"

"Bagel?" Kent followed him into the kitchen in a daze. He wondered if he'd stepped into the set of one of those ridiculous reality shows that Spencer had obsessively watched. "Why?"

"Best bagels in the Keys, right here. Don't get the French toast ones, they're odd." Dusk tilted the bag to allow the bagels to roll onto the table. "Well? What's your poison? I brought a variety."

"Cinnamon raisin."

His blue eyes seemed to stare through Kent's soul for long, uncomfortable seconds. "No? Really? I bet you'd prefer the asiago with bacon jam and a schmear of spiced cream cheese."

His mouth definitely didn't salivate, not even a little. *Okay, maybe a little drool had happened, but no one else needed to know.* "Bacon jam? Sounds intriguing."

Dusk crowed triumphantly, selecting the right one to shove into Kent's hands. "I knew it."

"Is insanity in the water?" Kent wondered how to get the barefoot animal doctor out of his kitchen without resorting to physical violence or calling the cops. "Why the hell are you here?"

"Work."

Kent could only stare stupidly at him. "Work?"

"I'm doing odd jobs around town to rebuild my clinic. You're *odd* and grumpy, and this place clearly needs to be repaired. I help, you pay."

He intended to refuse, but his dick sidetracked him with a more pertinent question. "Is your tongue pierced?"

"Yep. Want to touch?" Dusk's tongue darted out for a brief show-and-tell. "So? Want an extra set of hands?"

"If you can help me repair my cottage, why haven't you fixed up your clinic?" Kent sampled his coffee and had to clench his jaw to stop from releasing a happy moan. He did love a good cup of joe. His hippie intruder didn't need to know how *much* he enjoyed it. "Shouldn't insurance cover the cost of your rebuild? I would've assumed anyone who lives here would have hurricane coverage."

"Let me tell you all about the intricacies of insurance policies and how they screw you over."

Over the early morning breakfast, Dusk spoke about his troubles with his insurance company in an obviously much-abbreviated version. Kent had no doubts the story glossed over the actual depth of how much he had lost and how frustrating the situation must be. He found the younger man annoying, but offered him work despite his brain screaming at him to say no.

The quicker the cottage could be fixed up and sold for a profit, the sooner Kent would be able to begin to recover what he'd given away in his divorce settlement. An extra set of hands would make it go considerably faster.

"What's your clinic called?" His curiosity got the better of him.

"Dusk Til Dawn."

"Are you shitting me?"

"Nope."

"Were you high?"

"Not even a little," Dusk chuckled. "I'd never risk my patients, even if they are often furry and four-legged, by being impaired by anything, even sinus meds."

"I'll pay you for the day, and we can go from there." Kent saw no reason to rope himself into an on-going concrete agreement. "What can you do?"

He learned a valuable lesson then about how dangerous a single grin could be to his ability to maintain a cool head and a non-aroused dick. He failed badly on both counts. Dusk's smile did a number on him.

I blame the jewelry.

While Kent was mentally enjoying thoughts of pierced tongues, Dusk busied himself by cleaning up the crumbs from breakfast. He didn't even recall having finished his coffee, but lifting the cup only served to dump the lid in his face. *Smooth, very smooth.*

Wanting to recover his control, Kent retrieved the abandoned paper with his list. He would not test his restraint outside. Hot, sweaty bodies in the Florida sun? He had no intention of playing a starring role in his own personal B-grade porno flick, not that he'd ever watched one.

Nope, not me, except that one time.

His eyes flickered along the scribbles on the paper. "We might as well start in the kitchen."

Dusk peered around the room with a confused frown. "What's wrong with it?"

"Sink's cracked, pipes rattle, the linoleum has more bubbles than bubble wrap. I think the cabinets might be remnants from one of the world wars. They're warped enough to be that old." Kent ticked the flaws off on his fingers. "I'm not convinced the fridge didn't play host to a corpse of some sort for a while. It's rank."

An hour into stripping the cabinets out, Kent discovered the fatal flaw in his earlier thought process. Outside, there would've been sufficient space between them. In the kitchen, they worked cramped together. Not ideal.

Dusk had tossed his shirt aside early on, claiming to not want to ruin it with sweat. *Sure.* It left Kent with a constant eyeful of tanned, muscled, and tattooed flesh. He didn't know if it should motivate him to work faster or slower.

It had been a while since he'd spent hours bumping up against an incredibly attractive, younger man. He also whacked his thumb with a hammer for the first time in years. Dusk hadn't even attempted to hide his snickers at the cussing that followed.

None of it had been intentional, which made it worse. If Dusk had been trying to entice him, Kent could've gotten angry about it. Every touch or nudge seemed as innocent as the man himself.

The lumber arrived around noon, and Kent was grateful for the help in getting it stacked up beside the house. The truck driver didn't seem nearly as willing to assist. They managed it together, though it took over an hour.

Lunch had been surprising, like the rest of the day. Dusk insisted on treating Kent. He dragged them a few streets over to find the Beach Bites food truck, plying him with what turned out to be the best fish tacos *ever.*

They also stopped for chimney cakes from a

bakery in Mallory Square. The cinnamon- and sugar-covered funnels would keep him hopped up for at least a few hours. He hoped it would get him through the rest of the afternoon.

By the end of the day, the kitchen stood as bare as Dusk's upper body. They'd cleared out everything and even managed to prep the walls for paint. He would move on to the small living room, and then to the bedrooms, since it would be simpler to paint every-thing all at once.

"Tomorrow?" Dusk downed a bottle of water, holding it to his neck to cool himself off. He clutched his shirt in his other hand. Kent definitely *wasn't* watching the sweat roll down his chest. "Well, Mr. Grumpy? Can you put up with me for another day?"

Say no. Say. No. Can you really deal with this for another day? No. No, you can't.

"Sure. I could use the help."

Damn it. I'm a goddamn moron.

4

DUSK

"Saw you with the mountain man." Jesse saluted him with his beer when Dusk made it to his parents' bar late in the evening. "Did he give you a good workout?"

"You kiss your mother with that filthy mouth?" Dusk leaned across the bar to kiss his mom on the cheek and then slid onto a barstool. "I managed to work up a sweat today, stripping out the kitchen. Why mountain man?"

"Didn't you see the Colorado tags?"

His mom placed a plate of her homemade hummus and pita bread in front of him. "I wish you'd let us help you, honey. I hate seeing you so exhausted. We've got this place all fixed up again. Why not let us chip in a little?"

Jess bent forward to whisper, "Burgers later?"

"Don't you go corrupting my baby with your meat." She swatted him with a bar rag when he almost fell off his chair cackling. "I meant burgers."

Dusk choked on a piece of pita while laughing as the scolding continued. He decided to rescue the old beach bum. "Mom. Did you cook up any falafel today? I could eat a horse."

"One made out of tofu maybe," Jess threw in, earning another swat. "That's elderly abuse."

"She's older than you," Dusk pointed out helpfully.

"I'm eating your burger for that." Jesse reached out for his beer only to have it swiped away. "Well, I can see I've worn out my welcome."

"Since when?" Dusk teased lightly. "Meet you on the beach in an hour?"

"Yeah, yeah. You'll still be picking that sawdust out of your teeth." He gestured to the half-eaten hummus, wrinkling his face in disgust. "Keep the old bat away from me."

"Old bat?" His mom threatened Jesse with the empty bottle. "Old bat?"

Resting his arms on the weathered, wooden counter, Dusk allowed the familiar sounds of the bar to wash over him like a comforting blanket. The old icemaker vibrated almost loud enough to drown out

Miss Alice's evening karaoke attempts, which meant she hummed along to the tune in her head. He nodded in all the right places while his mother told him about her day, but his mind drifted away despite his best efforts.

It had been enjoyable working with Kent. Who wouldn't want to be holed up with an attractive man who handled power tools like a pro? He hadn't believed his luck when he'd basically tricked the man into a lunch date.

One of my better plans.

Miss Alice's constant offers notwithstanding, Dusk had enjoyed brief flings with visiting tourists over the last few years. None of the locals had ever gained his attention, so relationships tended to have the lifespan of the average vacation. He didn't mind, mostly; they practiced safe sex, had fun, and went their separate ways, mutually satisfied by the encounter.

His mind was drawn back to the sexy silver fox who he'd been cooped up with for an entire day. He'd almost taken a note from Miss Alice and swooned dramatically when Kent stretched and showed off his abdomen with the perfect sprinkling of gray hairs. It had made him want to drop to his knees and demonstrate the impressive finesse with which he could use his tongue ring.

Too soon? Definitely.

Aside from his flirtations, his one long relationship had involved a college professor. They'd dated for five years, through his time at veterinary school and his internship. Hearts had been broken, though, when Dusk had insisted on returning to Key West.

Neither Gainesville nor Jacksonville had captured his spirit like the Keys. The professor had given him an ultimatum. He hadn't responded well to the passive-aggressive attempt to guilt him into staying. Their romance had ended instantly, and not pleasantly.

Dusk had promised himself not to move into anything more than a fling unless the other person understood he wouldn't move for them. He'd suffered living on the mainland enough. He wouldn't leave his parents in any case, not with them getting older and frailer.

"Son?"

He started at the closeness of his dad's voice. "Yeah?"

"Jesse left a burger under the steps out back for you. Go on. I'll dance with your mother to distract her. You need more than chickpeas after the day you've had."

The burger had been cooked to sheer perfection.

Dusk waved to a few of the regulars, before making his way down to the beach. He sat to watch the sunset while enjoying the greasy, cheesy goodness. Jesse deserved a few beers for making the trip back to him.

He thanked his lucky stars that the apartment had been salvageable without much work. He hadn't enjoyed crashing on his parents' couch. His mom meant well, but her morning ritual of yoga and juice didn't cut it.

"Is it safe?"

He waved Jesse over to join him. "Thought you went home."

"Too early."

Dusk accepted the beer offered to him with a grin of thanks. "Burger was good."

"Better than sawdust?"

If his mother was one of the original hippies, Jesse might've been the mold from which Jimmy Buffet had been created. The only difference being the old beach bum sounded like a wounded dolphin when he attempted to sing. Dusk hoped one day to convince the man to share a bit about his life, more than the vague hints and tall tales.

A scraggly old timer who stumbled out of a life raft had to have a few good stories. Jesse always claimed not to remember any of the pertinent details. Dusk would keep trying, though, and maybe one day he'd either remember or finally share.

"What's mountain man's story?"

"No idea." Dusk had honestly been wondering the same thing, but hadn't wanted to pry. "It's possible he wanted to retire somewhere warm?"

"Nah. Man like that? He's got a story," Jesse nodded sagely. "Bet he lost all his money or something. He looks like he used to be rich. Bad investment? Or, maybe his wife took everything."

Wife? Not from the way his eyes stayed on my ass.

"I'm not interrogating the man to satisfy your curiosity." Dusk might do it on his own, at least to find out if he was single or even interested in men. "Don't even think about it. What did my mom tell you about minding your own business?"

"Why not?" Jesse kicked sand his way. "After all the effort I put into your clinic?"

"Asking me every five seconds to look at your shingles isn't effort." Dusk held his hand up to stop him when he immediately went to lift his shirt. "Still not interested."

"Did they teach you anything at school?"

"How to handle animals. You are not one, even if you act like it."

He let Jesse grumble into his beer and returned to

watch the last rays of the sun drift down past the horizon in the distance. The wind had kicked up the waves. The brilliant colors painted them in shades of gold and purple, making it a magical view for the last few minutes before twilight.

"Doesn't get old, does it?"

"Nope," Dusk grinned over at the older man. He could see a thousand and one sunsets across the ocean and find something unique about each one. "Hope it never does."

5

———

KENT

Sleep did not come easily to Kent. He closed his eyes only to be greeted by visions of tanned and toned skin, glistening in sweat and ripe for touching. Wet dreams. He hadn't had one of those since his college days.

The simple solution would've been to jack off, but it would only exacerbate the situation. If he caved now, it wouldn't be long before his nightly issue led him to ask Dusk out on a date. He refused to give in to what was clearly a midlife crisis.

What else could it be? His business had disappeared on him. His husband had left him for a younger man, and his dick had decided to hyperfocus on a barefoot lunatic masquerading as a vet. *I'm either having a midlife crisis, or I'm stuck in an episode of* The

Twilight Zone. He wasn't certain which would be better.

He started to doze off when the chickens began to cluck up a storm, sending him shooting out of bed and hunting for something to satisfy his sudden desire for KFC. "Damn things."

Halfway down the beach, toward the fleeing poultry, Kent realized perhaps putting on clothes might've been a wise idea. He stood naked in the pinkish hues of the rising sun, hoping he could get back to the cottage without anyone calling the cops. Running naked did *nothing* for the male anatomy.

"Forget something?" Dusk sat on his steps with two cups of coffee again, eyes drifting up and down without even a hint of embarrassment. "Didn't take you for a nudist."

Damn.

The intense stare shouldn't have caused a certain lower part to go from soft to standing at attention. Kent definitely shouldn't have enjoyed the spark of interest that flared in Dusk's eyes, darkening the blue hue considerably and causing the man to sit up a little straighter. He *should've* immediately moved inside to get dressed or maybe nap until the entire episode faded from his memory.

"I could help you with that." Dusk's lips turned up

into a grin made of pure silky sex. "With a hand? Or maybe a mouth?"

He has a tongue ring.

Random and unwanted, the thought struck him at the core of his self-control. His mind betrayed him cruelly with vivid flashes of Dusk demonstrating his particular talents. It didn't do a damn thing to help with his ever-growing problem.

Cold shower.

I need the iciest one I can find.

"Move your ass." Kent wanted to avoid brushing against him to get into the house. "I doubt the cops will appreciate my casually turning this into a nudist beach."

"Depends on the cop." He tilted his head to the side as if he wanted a better view. "They might have an appreciation for the artwork of the human form. I know I do."

"Get going."

"All right, keep your pants on—oh wait." Dusk slowly stood and managed to accidentally, on purpose drag his arm along Kent's body, making his shaft throb painfully. "Fuck-a-doodle-do. I'd love to help you resolve your wooden problem."

"I'll manage."

The low whistle, when Kent started up the stairs,

told him the younger man enjoyed both sides of his body equally. *Cold shower. Definitely time for one of those.* He would spend the time figuring out how to rid himself of the persistent pest who messed with his sleep and everything else.

Not jacking off. Maybe a little. No. I'm too old for bopping the baloney over some young thing.

A quick dip under a blast of frigid water got his brain back to where it should be—in the larger of his heads. He dressed and found Dusk settled in the mostly bare kitchen. Breakfast today involved coffee and coconut waffles from Camille's. The latter being a local and personal favorite apparently.

They tasted better than expected. He surprisingly didn't mind the company either. Dusk didn't mention his early morning streaking, but instead wanted to know more about his plans for the cottage.

While his initial plan for the day had been to work on the bedroom, Kent decided not to tempt fate. They cleaned everything out of the living room instead, even the furniture, loading it into the back of his Silverado, the one thing Spence hadn't taken from him. By evening, the only thing left to do inside was the one place he would prefer to handle alone.

He dined alone on the now repaired stairs at the back of the cottage, after having grabbed a burger from a food stand. He had a moment while watching a couple walking further down the beach to consider a text he'd received from his attorney.

Spencer is selling off all your properties.

Not super surprising. Kent had expected Spencer to quickly work at ridding himself of anything that might require maintenance. It had been part of their falling out of love—or his falling out in any case. He had discovered once they'd achieved a certain pinnacle of success that his husband no longer wanted to put in the long hours.

The days of working together faded into him alone putting in the hours instead at building sites. Kent had found, more and more frequently, the weight of every-thing on his shoulders. Spencer had been more than content to enjoy and spend the fruit of his labor.

I should've seen it coming.

Several of their friends had called him in the last few days, concerned about Spencer and his extreme spending. He'd bought one of the most expensive properties in downtown Denver and decorated it ostentatiously. Along with his boy toy, they had worked their way through flashy clothes, jewelry, and paying for lavish meals with friends.

Spencer would be in for a rude awakening when his wealthy living emptied the bank accounts. Even if he sold their entire real estate portfolio, Spencer could rapidly run through it all in a year easily, especially if he'd dropped a cool two million on a condo.

How did I miss the fact that I'd married a money-grabbing fool?

He found it hard to connect what his ex-husband had become to what he had been early on in their relationship. Spencer's parents were solid people who worked hard to put their son through college. They'd been quite possibly the most idyllic of families, which made the sudden change mystifying.

"You need ice cream."

Kent crushed the cup in his hand, spilling soda over himself when a familiar voice startled him out of his thoughts, which had grown morose. "Don't you have a life?"

"Yep, it involves taking you to Mattheeseen's." Dusk handled the bewildering name better than he would've. "You heard me."

"I did. I didn't understand shit, but I heard you." Kent found himself being dragged up to his feet unwillingly. "Aren't there other people here for you to harass?"

"Yes, but I haven't seen their John Thomas."

Okay. Fair point.

"Why ice cream?"

"Brain freeze should do you good." Dusk grabbed him by the arm to lead him up the beach to the road where two bicycles waited for them. "Hop on."

"No."

"What? Too old?" He asked mockingly.

"Old?" Kent allowed himself to be manipulated into riding the bike through the streets like a teenager and to the ice cream parlor, which was easily spotted by the bright red awning. "Mattheessen's?"

"Get the frozen key lime pie. It's orgasmic. Or the Cuban coffee ice cream, seriously." Dusk waved to a few of the people loitering outside with their own treats. "Well? Sugar waits for no man."

Stepping inside, Kent found himself assaulted by the sweet scent of all things sugary and creamy. Chocolate and some sort of fresh fruits added depth to the fragrance filling the place. He wondered if they'd ever considered bottling it—Eau de ice cream parlor.

Doesn't roll off the tongue, does it?

The key lime pie, frozen and dipped in chocolate, didn't quite strike his fancy. Kent had always loved deeper flavors, not the tart of citrus or berries. He opted for three scoops to give the place a fair assessment: black cherry, Cuban coffee, and dulce de leche in honor of his father's heritage.

With their treats in hand, Dusk led him, pushing

their bikes the almost mile down Southard Street to Fort Zachary Taylor. They managed the walk in an easy twenty minutes and sat on the beach to wipe up the last of the melted ice cream from their fingers. He expected the man to talk his head off, so the silence surprised him.

"Have plans for Thanksgiving?"

Kent hadn't thought much about the upcoming holiday. He would be avoiding his family meal; he'd had enough drama for one year. "None."

"Mom throws a dinner for all those who don't have a family to share the day with. It's tofu turkey and an all vegan-friendly menu." Dusk chuckled at the grimace of distaste Kent sent his direction. "Jesse and I usually sneak out to one of the local cafes that serve Thanksgiving dinner. You can join us."

"I can?"

"Shouldn't be alone this time of year. It's pathetic."

"Thanks."

6

————

DUSK

It had become clear over the course of the evening that Kent had wanted time alone. Dusk decided to focus his attention on visiting some of his usual clinic visitors to see how they were doing. It would let the man deal with whatever had him so lost in his thoughts.

As the end of November approached, Dusk knew some of the couples who lived in the Keys through the winter would start returning. He made sure to bike around to check on them. Many had older pets that he preferred to watch closely.

He also shared donuts and coffee with his dad. They'd missed the ritual for the last week, so the two men snuck out early to avoid his mom who preferred they have a healthier start to their day.

She meant well, but Dusk could remember with distaste some of her oatmeal experiments from his childhood. His father had begun the breakfast tradition then. He often wondered if she knew and pretended not to for their sake.

It had always been hard to sneak anything by his mother. She had eyes in the back of her head, and he wouldn't have her any other way.

The morning flew by with a menagerie of pets visited. He checked on turtles, a rabbit, three dogs, and several chickens. The snake stuck in a mattress had thrown him for a loop.

Reptiles.

During his internship, Dusk had learned many lessons on dealing with slippery reptiles. He genuinely loved most creatures. Snakes were definitely on the bottom of his list. He would never understand how some could adore them so greatly.

A young boy in the area named Adrian owned a young Hognose that had managed to get stuck in a hole in his bed. The family had been scared to dig him out. *Dr. Dusky to the rescue.* He worked his arm between the springs of the mattress, which would definitely need to be replaced, and pondered over his life choices.

Why did I want to be a vet again?

The sheer joy on Adrian's face when his beloved "Hoggy" was returned to him answered his unspoken question perfectly. Helping to reunite the little boy with his equally small snake made his day. He would normally have waved off the home visit fee, but the clinic wouldn't rebuild itself.

Dusk made his way across town on his bike, stopping to help one of his regulars whose cat had decided to give birth inside of a closet. Four adorable kittens delivered safely. He left the owner to watch over the nursing babies with a word of warning to call him if they showed any signs of illness—the first few days would be the hardest for the fluff balls.

With his non-human visits handled, Dusk decided to see how his parents' day had gone. Afternoons tended to be slower, as locals only showed up during lunch and evening hours. He ducked behind the bar and into the kitchen only to find his mother slaving away over vegetarian chili, and from the smells filling the room, cornbread as well.

"Hello, honey." She waved him over for a hug. "I've saved you some lunch."

"Tabbouleh salad, *yum.*" Dusk barely managed to hide his grimace.

"Dusk."

"Mom." He grinned innocently at her.

She shook her head at him. "You'll find your father out back playing around with his new generator."

"Insurance finally approved payment for it?"

"*Finally.*"

His folks had been battling with their adjuster for over a month. The repairs to the bar had been completed, but the generator hadn't been replaced. They kept it for rare times when the power went out during storms; it prevented food from spoiling and made life a lot more comfortable.

Kissing his mom on the cheek and snatching up some of her to-die-for cornbread, Dusk darted by her swinging spoon and headed out into the shed at the rear of the bar. His dad stood over a brand-new generator, cussing up a storm. He kicked the thing in apparent frustration.

"Not working?"

"Dusky." His father flung a manual at him. "See if you can make sense out of it. I'm not even sure it's in English."

"Looks like English."

"It's gibberish."

Dusk grinned at his dad, a man who had never been one to enjoy any sort of engine or technology. "And you think I'll do any better with it? I'm your son."

"You got your brains from your mother." He

popped the top on a can of beer and took a long drink from it. "I've been fiddling with the damn engine for two hours. What am I missing?"

"A mechanic?" He received a filthy bar rag in the face for his attempts at humor. "Why don't you call someone?"

"Waste of money." His dad kicked the thing again before hopping around for a second. "This is not groovy."

Dusk snorted in amusement and threw out a hand to steady the man. "Would you rather spend the money on someone to repair the generator or someone to heal your foot?"

"You get those smarts from your mother."

"True. I get my hate of technology from you." Dusk's cellphone was three years old and had a cracked screen. He kept paper files at the clinic which had made the water damage a real pain. "Want me to call someone?"

"I'll manage."

The words were dad-speak for, *I'll spend another day flinging tools, bad words, and my foot at the generator before Mom intervenes and calls in a professional.* Dusk had seen the same scenario happen repeatedly throughout his life. It was simply part and parcel of his parents' long-lasting romance.

"Son of a—"

Dusk lunged forward to catch his dad when he tripped over the toolbox on the ground. "Can I call for help now?"

"Don't tell your mother."

THE TWO WEEKS BEFORE THANKSGIVING FLEW BY. KENT had been surprised when Dusk only appeared on his steps every couple of days. Dusk seemed to have sensed Kent's growing frustration.

His assumption, that distance would lessen his undesired infatuation, proved to be wrong. He found constant reminders of the fluffy-haired Floridian everywhere. His boring breakfasts made in his now partly renovated kitchen lacked the zest of the other man. He never knew each morning what the paper sack would contain—donuts, bagels, burritos, or something completely foreign.

The order had been restored to his world. Whenever life grew chaotic, Kent had always been able to rely on work to settle everything down for him. He threw himself into the renovations with great success.

Over the course of ten days, Kent managed to finish the process of clearing out old furniture, damaged drywall, and ruined paint. He patched up water damaged spots and ripped up the carpeting. It gave him the perfect blank canvas for his vision of a beach house.

Replacing the drywall became his next priority. He would follow that up by putting in the wood floor, and then wrap up the work by painting in another month or so. He couldn't imagine the winter market for real estate was massive. A longer stay in Key West wouldn't be the end of the world.

I can always spend some time exploring the area with Dusk.

The day before Thanksgiving, Kent sat on his steps with coffee. His ritual each morning involved watching the sunrise and hoping to see the shaggy dog-walker. The latter, he steadily refused to admit to himself.

You're an idiot. An old fool. Divorced, broke, almost bankrupt, and you stink.

As pep talks went, his could definitely use a lot of work. The critical voice of dissent sounded remarkably like his family, same accents and cutting words.

He thought maybe the time had come to be kinder to himself, in his own head.

Setting his mug on the step next to him, Kent grabbed his cell phone to check his emails. His restless nights had only one positive aspect to them: ideas had been steadily coming to him in regards to ways to recover his losses. Messages had already gone out to a few of his old partners, ones who wouldn't have a conflict of interest with his ex-husband.

One incoming email caught his attention above all the others with the shocking title 'about your father.' *About my father?* He checked the '*to*' field and found his mother's name. *Damn it.* He didn't need family drama. Hadn't leaving Colorado been about avoiding it?

"You look like you need something stronger than coffee."

Kent had been so distracted by the words on his phone that he failed to notice the approach of the dog walker—who appeared to be without dogs to walk today. "Have any whiskey? I could use a gallon of it."

"Anything I can do to help?"

Innocent words, but for some reason, Kent stared up into those soulful, cobalt blue eyes and lost his mind. His hand shot out of its own accord to wrap around Dusk's wrist to drag him forward. He shifted his grip to the man's shirt, so he could then drag him down until they were practically nose to nose.

"Screw it," he muttered.

Slipping his calloused, work-scarred fingers into Dusk's soft hair, Kent yanked him into a rough kiss. Some first caresses were tentative greetings; he wanted to blast the door down with his lips. His sanity returned when a neighbor wolf-whistled at the pair of them.

He released Dusk's shirt—and lips, sinking back onto the step, breathing heavily with a bruised mouth and a hard shaft for his troubles. *What the hell do I say now?* He settled for an attempt at a mild, "morning."

Dusk snorted quietly while shaking his shirt to rid it of wrinkles. "Remind me to tell my mom to steer clear if you say hello like that."

"Don't stop on our account."

Kent pinched the bridge of his nose while the idiots next door continued to applaud and ask for an encore. "Maybe we should go inside?"

"You have work for me today?"

Kent's eyes were suddenly at the perfect level to notice the bulge in Dusk's board shorts. "I'll think of something to do with you."

"Will you?" He took a few steps forward, and the

bulge brushed against Kent's chin. "I bet I have a few ideas of my own."

Kent found his attention completely taken by Dusk's pierced tongue flicking out to lick swollen lips. It distracted him enough that he didn't immediately retaliate when the fabric covered anatomy was dragged across his face. "Ideas are good."

"Remember that demonstration I promised to give you? Ahh, you do remember," Dusk taunted. He stumbled backward down the hall, pulling Kent after him. "You might have to drop your trousers for this part."

Kent could think of multiple reasons why this counted as poor decision-making. He uttered an almost primal grunt instead and caught Dusk up in another searing kiss. His tongue demanded ownership of the other man's lips, brushing up against the surprisingly cool stainless steel ball, a sharp contrast to the sumptuous warmth of his mouth.

Their heated kisses lasted for long minutes, punctuated by short periods of jagged breathing. Their hands explored each other's upper bodies on top and underneath clothing, tracing over muscles and teasing nipples. The escalating passion led to T-shirts being ripped off and tossed absently to the side.

"You have scars." Dusk stated the obvious while

using one finger to feather across one of the many marks dotting Kent's arms and chest. "No ink?"

"I learned carpentry and construction the hard way. It comes with a price." Kent sucked in a fractured breath when Dusk kneeled to start mapping out those scars with his tongue, "You could say these are my tattoos."

"Inked by life?" Dusk met his eyes with a depth of understanding evident in his own. "I'm glad you stumbled around bare ass the other day."

"Oh?" Kent struggled to keep at least a portion of his brain functioning when the piercing bumped sensually against one nipple then the other. He steadied his out-of-control breathing with measured inhales and exhales, allowing him to sound somewhat unfazed. "Why?"

Dusk reached out boldly to wrap his supple fingers around the hardening shaft in Kent's shorts. "I already know what you have underneath here. No disappointing surprises to worry about. I've been looking forward to this for days."

Any thought of responding died instantly when that molten-hot mouth drifted down his well-defined abs. Dusk's nimble fingers made quick work of the button on his shorts while his tongue explored the coarse gray hairs revealed when the clothing dropped to the floor.

"Damn." Kent bucked up against the teasing. "What the hell are you doing there?"

"If it isn't obvious, you've gone without for a long time."

Warm air wafted across his aroused flesh. Dusk smirked up at him, puffing out exaggerated breaths to toy with the man. Kent grabbed the edge of the nearby doorframe to ensure he could remain standing through the onslaught.

Kent learned several valuable lessons over the course of the next few minutes. Dusk had not exaggerated his abilities with his tongue. His knees weren't as strong as they used to be. And unfinished floors hurt like the dickens when his legs gave out.

The laughter from Dusk didn't last long. He swung his body around after shucking off his board shorts. His dick bumped against Kent's lips while his mouth returned to its languorous devouring of the older man's shaft.

Not to be outdone, Kent maintained enough mental capacity to show off his own abilities. Dusk might manipulate with his tongue and piercing seductively and playfully, but Kent tended toward strong flicks and a commanding pace. They turned it into a competitive sport, testing to see who could push the other over the edge first.

The sound of the waves outside was punctuated by moans and all the cacophony that came with the skilled expression of oral pleasure. They lifted up at the end, exchanging mouths for firms hands, leaving their chests splatted with the evidence of their success.

"Damn." Kent collapsed on the unfinished floor, wincing when his head hit a stack of the wood flooring yet to be installed. "Shower?"

"What? No skinny-dipping in the ocean?" Dusk slowly got to his feet and held out a hand to help the older man. "That shower big enough for two?"

The flush of ecstasy had faded into the harsh light of practicality. Kent had engaged in sexual gratification with a man he'd known for less than a second. It went against his usually pragmatic and cautious approach to life. He thought maybe it could be another oddity chalked up to his midlife crisis.

Yes, that sounds right. So, why do I still want to ask him into the shower? And maybe out for brunch?

Damn it.

8
———

DUSK

THE AWKWARDNESS DUSK FEARED MIGHT INJECT ITSELF into the morning never quite appeared. He observed the older man while kneeling side by side to install the wooden floors. It didn't take an overly observant person to see he'd reached some internal limit.

His eyes were drawn and weary. Kent hadn't laughed at a single joke. He'd become consumed by the desire to finish the renovation, or at least throw himself into it.

"You are in desperate need of a break." Dusk sat on his heels and snatched the tool out of the other man's hands. "Can you swim?"

"What? Why?" Kent frowned when he refused to elaborate. "Yes, I can swim."

"Put on your Speedo. We're going out." Dusk

ignored the spluttering indignation coming from behind him about "not owning a damn Speedo" and gave one of the Key West kayaking tour companies a call. "Ahoy! Captain Tess?"

"Dusky."

"So, remember when I snip snipped your Captain Whiskers' willy for free?" He held the phone away from his ear when she laughed loudly. "What are your plans for the day? How about snorkeling at the refuge and a sunset picnic on the boat?"

"Whiskers has a thing on his stomach."

"Fine, fine, I'll check Captain Whiskers for the lump that I've already told you is fatty tissue you don't have to worry about."

"Are you sassing me?"

"No, ma'am, I would never sass you."

"You'd sass an undertaker," Tess shot back. "And you're fixing the picnic for yourself. I ain't got time to make dinner for you."

"I wouldn't want to eat it. You burn toaster waffles."

"Don't worry, Dr. Dusky. I'll tell you what. How about I have my cabin boy throw something fancy together for you?" She gave another braying laugh which as always surprised him, since it didn't fit her petite, but stocky body. "Your guest have any allergies?"

"None. I'm telling Hope you called her a cabin boy." Dusk's stomach had already begun to growl at the thought of food from Tess's wife, Chef Hope, from one of the most acclaimed restaurants in all of South Florida. "And Tess? Thanks."

"Anytime."

He dropped his phone into his pocket and turned to find Kent hadn't moved an inch. "Well? Hop to it, unless you want me to dress you."

"I'm too busy."

Dusk refused to allow the man to sink further into his funk. "Nope. Not hearing it. If you don't join me today, I'll let chickens loose in your cottage every day at four in the morning until you do agree to it."

"I'll deep fry them."

"With all the secret spices?" He swallowed a shout of triumph when he surprised a smile out of the brooding man. Kent pressed his lips tightly into a thin line. "If Speedos aren't your thing, how about a thong? You've got the butt for it."

"Did you…?"

Dusk redirected Kent across the living room into the bedroom. "Bring a towel and a jacket. A breeze might kick up on us."

"You aren't trying to take me out into a storm are you?"

"Nah."

He trusted Tess completely. She wouldn't risk her boat or their lives if the weather stood a chance of turning ugly. From the clear skies earlier, they'd likely have the perfect conditions to explore all the ocean had to offer.

An hour later, they loitered around the marina awaiting the arrival of Captain Tess Rogers and her aptly named boat, The Jolly Regina. Dusk had occupied his time wisely, ogling the tanned, dark-hair-covered, toned legs that belonged to the man in front of him. It was noon, and the sun highlighted Kent's southern Spanish ancestry.

One of his classmates in college had been incredibly proud of his Spanish family, and Dusk noticed similarities in the olive tint to his skin, which was perhaps a shade darker than his friend's. His tawny eyes were similarly deep-set, but Kent's stood out nicely against his graying hair. His distinct nose didn't detract at all from his looks, only sharpened them.

"Something in my teeth?" Kent had definitely grown tired of his blatant perusal. "Where the hell are we going?"

"Out there." Dusk pointed in the general direction of the refuge. "Or maybe, to the east a bit."

The putt-putt of the boat engine stopped any further questions. Dusk led the way down the walkway and waited for it to come closer before hopping easily onto the back of it. He turned to give Kent a hand if necessary. Tess waved cheerfully at the both of them.

Putting the boat in reverse, Tess went through her normal safety spiel for Kent's benefit. Dusk, having heard it all before, turned his attention to the massive, fluffy, orange tabby prowling freely on the boat. As expected, the cat was in perfect health, if not in need of a bit more exercise.

The Key West National Wildlife Refuge covered over three hundred square miles of beautiful, protected habitat. Some areas were inaccessible to prevent erosion and damage to the incoming migrating birds. It still offered some of the most peaceful and enjoyable spots for shallow water exploration.

After a quick snorkeling lesson, Dusk led Kent through some of the seagrass meadows. They swam for close to two hours, taking their time to see the various sea creatures that called the refuge home. He had always loved going out there.

When they returned to The Jolly Regina, Dusk felt a sense of pride at having eased some of the tension in Kent's face. The man had definitely enjoyed himself. They were tired, but satisfied—always a good sign.

The wind picked up on the return trip, enough to warrant pulling on jackets. Tess moored the boat behind one of the mangrove forests, and she retrieved several plates from the cooler to set on a chest between the benches at the back.

Refusing their invitation to eat, Tess grabbed her cat and ducked below deck. It left them to dine and watch the sun drifting down in the evening sky. Hope had outdone herself with seviche and several other cold appetizers along with a chilled bottle of wine.

Kent stretched his arm out to catch him by the hand. "Thanks. I've enjoyed myself."

"First time in a while you've let yourself?" Dusk asked observantly.

The food was forgotten briefly. Dusk followed the tugging fingers to straddle Kent's legs on the cushioned bench. His hands gripped those steady shoulders, and their eyes met for heated seconds until they gave in to the need for their lips to connect.

"No screwing around on the boat," Tess yelled from inside.

"What about the time—"

"No screwing around on the ship if you aren't the captain and her first mate," Tess corrected herself.

"Oh, hey, Hope got promoted."

"Eat your dinner." Tess rejoined them to wag a finger at him in warning. "Behave, or I'll tell your mom you eat meat."

"Yes, Captain."

"I'd like you to eat my meat." Kent lifted his hips up.

"Later." Dusk winked at him.

9

———

KENT

THANKSGIVING ARRIVED WITH KENT HAVING TO MUTE calls from both his mother and his ex-husband. He had yet to look into the email about his father. Pandora's Box didn't always have to be opened; it couldn't be unseen once read, and he wasn't ready.

Holidays always brought drama, or they had for the last few years. He would happily bury his head in the sand to not deal with any of it. He clung to his coffee and turned his phone off.

Problem solved.

He started to contemplate scraping together some sort of breakfast when a familiar whistle came from outside, followed by a tapping on the back door. "It's open."

Dusk strolled in casually and dropped a box in

front of him. "Pumpkin donuts, ginger spice muffins, and cranberry coffee cake, take your pick. I raided the bakery for us."

Us?

Kent found a frosted orange donut shoved under his nose. "Smells like pie."

"Hence the name." Dusk snagged a muffin for himself before twisting a chair around, straddling it, and resting his arms along the back. "Ready for turkey dinner?"

"Don't you mean Tofurky?"

Dusk wrinkled his nose in distaste. "Me eating meat is the worst kept secret in the Keys, but it makes Mom happy to make her vegetarian feast."

"And you love her?"

His blue eyes softened with emotion. "Mom taught me how to be kind and patient. She showed me how to soothe injured animals. She's an amazing woman."

"Who keeps feeding you flavored Styrofoam?"

"Basically," Dusk grinned. "You are coming, right? I promise the real turkey dinner later more than makes up for it."

Wiping his hands on a napkin, Kent resisted the temptation to have a third pastry. He shut the lid on the box and glanced at the younger man expectantly. It might be entertaining to watch someone else's family drama instead of slogging through his own.

Dusk shoved the remainder of his muffin into his mouth and grabbed the box of treats. "Shall we?"

Opting not to cycle when invited to, Kent redirected the shaggy-haired vet toward his truck. He chose to disregard the protests about wasting gas for a ten-minute ride. The holidays were a time of excess, or maybe that had just been Spencer's idea of it.

"I don't give a damn. I'm too tired to cycle around like I'm in the Tour de France. I don't have the legs for it anyway." He hopped into his truck, waiting for the man to put the bikes in the back and join him. He put his Silverado into reverse and backed out of the drive. "Let's go."

"Are you always lazy on Thanksgiving?" Dusk asked before holding his head out the window of the truck to yell at a man on the sidewalk. "Dinner at six?"

"Seven."

Dusk dropped back into his seat. "He's the chef at the café. He deep fries turkeys. So. Good. I'll have to sneak some in for Dad after, maybe in a sandwich."

"Why don't you tell your mom you'd rather not choke down tofu?" Kent wasn't sure he had the dedication to do it every year. "I would."

Dusk only shrugged in response.

They arrived at the bar, cutting the conversation short. He found Dusk's parents exactly how he imagined them. His mother wore a flowing dress with wooden bangles and had wild, curly gray hair. His father looked almost identical to him aside from being almost bald and having a body bent with age.

They welcomed him with open arms. He found a harvest ale placed in his hand—another tradition apparently. The family had many of them.

Thanksgiving with his mother and her family had been a stiff, formal occasion. Even as a child, he'd been forced into a suit and tie. Hands were held for prayer before a bite of food could be eaten.

It had never been a pleasurable experience. His cousins took great enjoyment in teasing him, goading him into responding to get him in trouble. It was likely the reason he had never complained about the over-the-top celebrations Spencer threw for all of their friends.

His expectations for the day, understandably, had never been high. Dusk and the patchwork family at the Barefoot Saloon had greatly surprised him. The day went more like the Publix ads on TV that he had always mocked for being overly dramatic.

The tables inside the bar had been dragged outside to the patio and shoved together to fit everyone. Aside from the slightly suspect pretend meat, he greatly enjoyed the other vegetarian dishes. The roasted carrots, French bread stuffing with onions and swiss chard, stuffed acorn squash, and mashed sweet potatoes were all delicious.

Dusk sat across from him at the absurdly long table and lifted his own beer bottle to salute him. "Happy Thanksgiving."

Milling around after the meal, Kent noticed several people eying him up. One of them, Jesse, finally approached him and sat beside him. He sipped the mild ale and waited for the questions to start.

It didn't take long.

"So, Dr. Dusky brought you?" Jesse continued gruffly not offering a chance for Kent to respond. "He's got a good heart. Treats animals and people well, even if he won't look at my spots."

Kent didn't know if a specific answer was required. He picked at the label on the bottle in his hand to give himself time to consider. "Do you have a lot of spots?"

He cackled loudly, pounding Kent on the back good-naturedly. "You hurt the doctor, and I'll drown you in the ocean so deep they'll never find your body."

"Sounds fun." Kent wondered how to take a death threat from a man who looked like the poster boy for beach bums from the late sixties. "Shouldn't this be coming from Mr. Keller?"

"They'll be too busy feeding you moist sand and fried sponge." Jesse's smile reminded him a little too much of a hyena he'd seen in a zoo. "It wouldn't be the first time I buried a body at sea."

He didn't find that bit of information surprising. "Do you always reserve threats for after Thanksgiving dinner?"

"Reserve 'em for folks who deserve 'em." Jesse bent forward in his chair with a glint in his cloudy, gray eyes. "You don't want to be one of those."

"Are you being ornery, Jesse?" Mrs. Keller walked over with her hands on her ample hips. "Don't listen to the old reprobate, Kent. We haven't gotten a lick of sense out of him since he washed up out of the ocean."

Any thoughts of dismissing the man outright faded at the iron in his eyes. Whoever Jesse had been in his previous life, he hadn't been a man to cross. He also wouldn't be likely to take kindly to someone poking around in his past, no matter how enticing the mystery surrounding him might be to solve.

While Jesse wandered over to Mr. Keller, Kent allowed Dusk to drag him into an impromptu game of touch football on the beach. They abandoned the game to the others after a while. He walked further down the sand with the always barefoot veterinarian who pulled out a Frisbee much to his amazement.

In college, Dusk had become involved in a Frisbee league. Kent laughed until the skill of the younger man had him stumbling around to catch the disk. He failed with embarrassing frequency until he caught on to the rhythm of it.

Several hours flew by pleasantly under the cloudy sky, tossing the Frisbee back and forth. All too soon, they had worked up their appetites. Dusk had him take the long way off the beach, skirting around the bar to reach the truck without being seen by his mother.

Laughing like teenagers with the munchies, they made their way a few blocks over to one of the few restaurants open over the holiday for a more traditional meat-filled repast. The café was packed with people, all looking for the comforting warmth of a turkey dinner. None of them left hungry or disappointed.

Stuffing their faces with all the familiar favorites, a quiet hum of satisfaction settled over everyone. Soft, instrumental music covered the clinking of silverware against china. The homey scents of buttered bread, gravy, and pies enticed their stomachs further.

"Is it worth it?" Dusk asked after making short

work of his first serving. "Save room for their key lime cheesecake and bourbon chocolate pecan pie. I've had wet dreams about them all year waiting for a first taste."

"I'm not sure if I should be aroused or nauseated." Kent laughed at the exaggerated lusty moan Dusk directed at the perfectly fried, crispy turkey skin on his plate. "I'm going with mildly disturbed."

"You or me?"

"I'm not sure. Are you going to eat that?" Kent watched with morbid fascination as his dinner partner made oral love to his fork. "Should I leave you alone with your poultry?"

Dusk crunched his way happily through the mountain of turkey he'd built on his plate. "My mouth is capable of handling a variety of meats. No need for yours to be jealous."

"Yep. I'm sticking with disturbing." He wouldn't admit to a slight hint of hypocrisy in his teasing, given the speed in which he'd cleaned his own plate. "Best Thanksgiving dinner I've had in a long time."

"Yeah?" His hopeful blue eyes shot straight through him. "So good?"

"More than." Kent's heart contracted painfully when that sharp gaze pierced his. "Best holiday I've had in ages that didn't require at least two bottles of Jack to get through."

"I'm—" Dusk trailed off into a hushed worshipful murmur when the server brought around a tray. "Pie."

"You worry me."

Afternoon faded into twilight, night finally fell, and Kent couldn't recall ever feeling quite so full of food. He'd almost had to roll himself and Dusk out to the truck. They made one stop to the bar to stow a plate under the steps for Mr. Keller.

Not sure that's sanitary.

With a six-pack of beer, Dusk led Kent to a hidden away beach no one frequented. They sat in the cool sand, counting stars and belching the alphabet. *Oh, we're classy.* He couldn't imagine his family or his ex-husband indulging in anything so sophomoric, no matter how fun.

One hour. Two beers. One shooting star. One roaming crab. One sexy Frisbee-throwing vet.

All random parts that collectively made up what Kent found himself grateful for at this time of year. Kent had left his shoes in the truck and dug his toes into the sand. Dusk leaned against him, pointing out another constellation.

Kent blinked when a square foil packet smacked

into his nose and dropped into his lap. He picked it up, squinting in the dark. *A condom?* "Is this a hint?"

"The condom?" Dusk kneeled in front of him, hands slithering up Kent's legs into the bottoms of his shorts. "No, this is the hint."

His fingers that had been cooled by beer were a sharp contrast to the warmth between his thighs. Kent inhaled sharply when they strayed into his boxers. Not waiting for an invitation, Dusk massaged him, bringing his arousal to full attention.

"I'm ready."

Kent stammered, caught off guard by Dusk already having the condom wrapper between his teeth to open it. "Ready?"

"Lubed and plugged."

Well, damn.

"I thought nurses were naughty, not doctors—or vets." His dick could've poked a hole through titanium; Dusk's admission had stiffened him painfully. "How long have you been ready?"

"Remember when I disappeared into the bathroom at the bar earlier?" Dusk ground himself along Kent's bent knee, still fighting with the foil packet. "I've been waiting for this all day, though."

His heart beat so hard in his chest that Kent thought it might deafen him. He watched in the moonlight while Dusk stripped both of them down to nothing. His shaft throbbed interestedly when the condom was skillfully rolled down it.

Turning around in front of him, Dusk kneeled in the sand, spreading his cheeks and took the plug to push it in and out. Kent struggled not to shoot his weapon prematurely. He wanted to savor the moment.

Screw savoring it.

He moved aggressively forward, taking the toy from Dusk. He mercilessly thrust it several times before replacing it with himself. The air seemed to sizzle around them as he sank into the younger man's exquisite heat.

Dusk dropped his head on his arms and rolled his hips with an exasperated groan. "Use it or lose it."

"No threatening when I have you by the balls." Kent reached around to roll them expertly in his fingers, eliciting a breathy grunt from Dusk. "Ready?"

"Yes, for fuck's sake."

His body thrummed with eager anticipation while he absently traced the lines of the Florida map on Dusk's back. He waited for an impatient whine to begin pounding into the lube-slicked man. From their fractured breathing, neither of them would be lasting long.

No wonder if he's been stimulating himself all afternoon.

"Shit. Just. Like. That." Dusk grabbed fruitlessly at the sand to support himself. "Harder, God, more please."

Grabbing him by the hips hard enough to bruise, Kent answered his begging with forceful and sharp thrusts. A brutal pace which he couldn't hope to keep up for long. He lost himself in the frenzied pace, so the sudden clenching from Dusk's release caught him entirely off guard.

His legs buckled and caused him to drop forward onto Dusk, pressing him into the sand while he roared out his own crescendo. He gasped for air afterward. "Damn."

Dusk grinned at him moments later when they lay side by side, staring up at the stars. "I've got sand in unpleasant places."

"I have—what the shit?" Kent shot up off the beach with a pained yelp to find a creature dangling between his legs. "I've apparently got crabs or one crab."

Dusk collapsed into tears of laughter while Kent plucked the crustacean free and let it scurry off. "It's not a Florida vacation without crabs."

10

DUSK

AN ITCHY TRUCK RIDE TO THE COTTAGE LED TO DUSK
convincing Kent to double up in the shower. *So much
sand in so many uncomfortable places.* He caught the
builder by the arm to drag him into the standing stall
which had plenty of room for both of them. The
condoms burned a hole in his pocket when he tossed
his shorts to the floor.

Soaping up his hands once they stood naked under
the warm water, Dusk tortured himself and Kent by
slowly roaming over every inch of the man's wet
olive-toned flesh. His fingers plucked nipples, dragged
along muscles, and dipped along the crease of his
behind.

With the detachable shower head, Dusk rinsed
away all the sand and suds. He took up the soap for a

second time to start the next phase of his plan. Kent grabbed onto the safety bar unsteadily when a slick finger tapped underneath his balls and strayed further along the sensitive skin.

"Soap stings," Kent said with what sounded like personal experience. "Not a complaint, an observation."

"You enjoy it." Dusk already knew the answer from the spongy head bumping against his forehead. "You do. Good. You'll love this."

Steam engulfed the room while hot water battered against them and the tiles relentlessly. Lusty, rough sighs mixed with the staccato of the shower. Dusk heard none of it while centering his attention on shallow thrusts of one then two fingers into Kent.

After rinsing off the soap once again, Dusk first nuzzled his nose against the dripping member before lapping at the head with his tongue. He nipped gently at it with his teeth, enjoying the hiss of approval from Kent. One quick move had the shaft engulfed by his mouth and gliding into his throat.

"God. Damn." Kent's fingers gripped his hair harshly. "Damn your mouth. I'm going to—"

"Not yet." Dusk clamped his fingers tightly around the base of his arousal. "Not so easily."

They tumbled relatively safely out of the bathroom

into the bedroom. Not worrying about making the sheets damp, Dusk shoved Kent onto the bed. He sucked a drop of water from the man's nipple, grinning before lifting himself up to press his swollen lips against the older man's.

The first kiss was almost chaste, a simple peck of their mouths. Tongues met with the second. By the third, their hands had begun to feverishly explore their still wet bodies.

Sloppy kisses turned into lip biting and tongue sucking. Dusk searched blindly for the lube and condoms that had been casually discarded on the way to the bed. It took longer to find because he didn't want to surrender the prize of Kent's mouth.

"Found it." Dusk held the items in his hand triumphantly. He ran his hand lazily down the center of Kent's chest, flicking his fingers against his side. "Yes? Say yes."

One hand idly kneaded Kent's erection while his other returned lubed fingers to his sought-after treasure. He'd already stretched the man; this was more to draw out the moment. He playfully teased the already aroused body underneath him.

Holding out for when he could see the desire in Kent's eyes reach a feverish peak, he slipped on the condom and inched himself forward. His pace drew a frustrated curse from his sensual captive.

Their time on the beach had been rushed and frenzied. Dusk wanted to show the joy of slow lovemaking. He would wring out every inch of ecstasy possible, drive them both to the highest plateaus of satisfaction.

More importantly, Dusk had a savage need to make a powerful statement with his skill. Like mellow bourbon on a hot summer day, he drank in Kent's essence with each calculated penetration. The older man's fingers clawed at the mattress, bunching the sheets up while he met each thrust.

They made love lazily on the wet sheets. Dusk worked hard to guide them both to an almost simultaneous completion. They held each other's gaze long after the electricity between them faded away.

"The sheets are wet."

Wet sheets turned out to be as uncomfortable as wet sand. They got themselves cleaned up and changed the bed, collapsing on it with exhausted grunts afterward. He fell into an almost immediate dead sleep.

Their sleep was deep and prolonged. Dusk awoke to find himself alone in bed. Sounds in the kitchen told him Kent had decided to make something to eat.

For the first time since they'd met, Dusk wouldn't be bringing in food from one of the many local restaurants. It had become a bit of a tradition almost, bringing new treats to entice Kent. He played the part of a true southern gentleman, well, as southern as any Floridian considered themselves to be. He sniffed appreciatively at the scent of bacon.

He couldn't contain a massive grin at the plate of bacon in the center of the kitchen table. "You speak my language."

"Hog?" Kent held up a carton of eggs to catch his attention. "Scrambled or complicated?"

Dusk choked on the piece of bacon he'd been in the process of inhaling, hacking and coughing to clear his throat. "Complicated? How exactly do you make eggs complex?"

"You'll see."

He learned quickly how complicated eggs could get if one didn't know how to cook them beyond swirling them around. He peered over Kent's shoulder at the stove. "What is that?"

"Sunny side up?" Kent scratched the underside of his jaw and jiggled the rubbery gunge in the pan. "So, scrambled?"

"*Definitely.*"

For a man who could turn a fried egg into a

horror-movie-worthy mess, the scrambled eggs tasted almost heavenly. Kent refused to discuss the great gulf between the two extremes of his abilities in the kitchen. He had a sly way of redirecting the conversation without appearing to have changed it.

The one dark shadow on the morning had been the ever-present ringing of Kent's phone. Dusk tried to ignore it. He really did. His curiosity had him itching to know who kept dialing over and over, trying to reach the man so desperately.

After the tenth attempt, Kent stepped out of the room with an apology. Dusk generally considered himself a well-mannered person, but he couldn't help straining his ears to hear a part of the hushed argument or at least one side of it. The older man returned to the table after ten minutes with a broken phone and a face like a hurricane.

"Good talk?" Dusk went with the obvious. He picked up a section of the destroyed cell phone. "Did you decide to give it a time-out?"

"A permanent one," Kent snorted. "My ex-husband can be persistent."

"Ah, ex-tra drama you might say?"

"Clever."

"Do you want to talk about it?" Dusk offered, expecting and receiving a refusal. He wouldn't have wanted to air his dirty relationship laundry either. "What's on the books for today?"

"For us?" Kent lifted graying eyebrows. "I'm hoping to make significant progress with painting. It's perfect weather to have the windows open to air it out."

"Painting it is." He chugged down the last of his now cold coffee. "I'll work for free today."

While perusing the colors, Dusk had to react quickly to catch the old radio flung his direction. Kent told him to find something "not idiotic" to listen to as they worked. He ignored the popular stations. After several minutes of fiddling with dials, Tush by ZZ Top blared out of the speakers.

Ahh, the classics.

Two cans of a blue-gray paint pretentiously called *Quiet Moments* later, they had made good progress on not only the bedroom and den but kitchen as well. The effort and the paint speckles in their hair had been worth it.

Another shared shower led to Kent taking Dusk against the tile wall. He returned the favor, bending the builder over the sink. They'd required a second rinse by the time they collapsed exhausted on the bathroom rug, used condoms discarded in the wicker trash can in the corner.

They had intended to head out for dinner. Exhaustion caught them off guard. Sleep claimed their tired bodies, barely giving time to ensure the windows had been closed.

Growling stomachs woke them up the following morning. Dusk decided not to risk another questionable egg experience. He dragged Kent out to the Cuban Coffee Queen for breakfast sandwiches and iced café con leche, best in Florida.

Seeing one of his clients across the way, Dusk left Kent to jog over to catch up with the man. He returned to find his breakfast buddy scowling at him. *Curious.* He watched those work-calloused fingers rip a napkin to shreds.

"Who's that?"

Dusk peered at him as the huffing and shredding suddenly made sense. "You're jealous."

"Not even close."

"Yep, you are. First, allow me to laugh at you, considering we've known each other for barely a month and could only even loosely count having gone on a handful of dates at this point. Second, you should be aware the man you are jealous over is named Carlos. He is asexual, heteromantic, and happily married to his wife, Penny, and as likely to want in my pants as Jesse is. So not even remotely likely to happen." Dusk reached over to grab the last chunk of

Kent's sandwich. "I'm eating yours by way of punishment."

"I wasn't jealous." Kent crossed his arms and frowned at him. "Can I have my sandwich?"

"Nope." Dusk shoved the remaining bit into his mouth and grinned around it. "Another coffee?"

11

———

KENT

Mid-December

WINTER NEVER TRULY ARRIVED IN THE KEYS. KENT found the mild temperatures enjoyable, but he did miss the snowy days of Colorado, not the shoveling and driving in the icy mess, though. He thought maybe retirees who moved south had the right idea.

As Christmas drew closer, his mood took a nose-dive. He channeled it into renovations. *Typical.* Construction, building anything with his hands had always been therapeutic for him.

He enjoyed demolition, sure, what hot-blooded man didn't. Turning the empty shells into a beautiful home appealed to him even more than destroying them. It reminded him of a phoenix rising from the ashes. Old houses deserved second chances, unlike people.

At the height of his success with flipping houses, Kent often donated several each year to homeless veterans or single mothers. He'd taken great pride in offering help not many could. Spencer hadn't understood his throwing profits away.

How did I not see the signs?

Too late now.

Motivated by his desire to forget, the renovations of the small cottage had shifted into warp speed. Painting, both inside and out, had been completed two weeks ahead of schedule. The cabinets had been replaced, floors installed and finished; now he only had to add the decorative details that would make it a home.

Coffee in hand, Kent poured over the offer forwarded to him by a local realtor interested in the cottage for a client. The price far exceeded his initial hopes for selling the place. The sweat and blood put into the repairs had obviously done their job.

He would sell, take the funds to buy additional hurricane-damaged properties, repeating the process again. His business didn't have to falter forever. He could repeat his accomplishments without interference from his ex-husband.

He could bring himself back to life.

One more sip of coffee and back to it.

He didn't bother getting up when someone knocked on the front door. Dusk had promised to come by after his usual dog walking. "It's open. Coffee's on."

"How do you stand this—hovel? I know you enjoy flipping houses, but do people honestly dream of owning homes of this sort? I have a closet larger than this." Spencer's voice filled the room with all its familiar sharp edges and merciless aim, leaving nowhere to hide. "Say hello, Kent. I've actually flown economy to see you. I'm sure I'll contract Zika. Do mosquitos bite in the winter? Well? Aren't you thrilled to see me?"

"*Thrilled,*" Kent deadpanned. Spencer had once been able to send his heart racing, now it plunged into his stomach. "I usually call the cops on uninvited guests."

"Kent, be a doll, get me a cup of coffee?" Spencer looked sideways at the kitchen chairs before sitting in one. His designer suit fit his body perfectly, and he knew it. "I've missed you."

"Bullshit." He ignored the demand for coffee and focused on his ex-husband fully. "Why are you here? You hate Florida."

"I *missed* you," Spencer repeated slowly, enunciating each word.

The impatient tone to the supposedly warm sentiment didn't jive at all. He waited. It didn't take long. Spencer had never been patient even when his other flaws had been masked by a quick laugh, a handsome face, and a seemingly open heart—too open in the end.

"What happened to your, sorry, can't remember his name, the barely legal midlife crisis you were screwing in our bed?" Kent watched the emotions flicker across his former partner's face—guilt, anger, and annoyance most prominently. "What happened to us? We were happy, weren't we?"

"You worked too much."

"You spent too much."

"So did you." Spencer canted his head to one side. "You made me seem shallow. All the charity work, Habitat for Humanity, giving away houses left and right. No one enjoys having their face shoved in someone else's good deeds. You made me feel guilty for enjoying my hard-earned money."

"Why didn't you help me with it then?"

"I gave money to charities. They didn't need my time as well."

In those words, Kent found the crux of the failure of their marriage. The starting point. The fracture which began the slow collapse. Spencer threw cash at everything, taking the easy way out whenever possible.

Once had become twice and then ten times; Kent had always preferred to avoid the easy way. His ex-husband had grown too accustomed to their bank account solving problems. They'd fought about it often.

"You made me feel small." Spencer's obsidian eyes held a haunted vulnerability. "I disappointed you. The things, the men, they brought me joy when you didn't."

"I made you?" Kent noticed how it all seemed to be something he had done to Spencer. He couldn't help shaking his head at the lack of insight. "The divorce is finalized. You have the house and the bank account. You sold the business. Why are you here?"

"Why are you in such a hurry to get me to leave? Are you afraid of facing your mistakes? Isn't that why you signed everything so quickly?" Spencer sniped at him.

"You fucked him in our bed." Kent's patience snapped like an overstretched rubber band. "What more can I possibly give that you haven't already taken?"

"You've done well with this." He blithely ignored the irate sneer sent his direction and slowly glanced around the kitchen. "The hurricane damage seemed almost unrepairable when *we* originally bought it. I'm impressed. You always had an amazing gift for renovating."

We?

"Running low on funds?" Kent smiled sharply. He suddenly had an idea of what prompted the visit and it definitely had nothing to do with any sort of reconciliation. "How much have you lost?"

"William emptied the bank account." Spencer averted his eyes to the tabletop. "Don't laugh."

"Why not? You chuckled when I signed it all over to you." Kent pressed his lips together to stem the sudden sickening weight in the pit of his stomach. It horrified him to think of all of his hard-earned wealth being squandered away in less than a year. "What about the penthouse?"

"Selling it."

"Cars?"

"Sold," Spencer repeated the word dully.

"What on earth did you do with it all?"

"Whatever I wanted until William stole it all." Spencer had a hopeful expression in his eyes, only slightly tainted by the manipulative gleam he could also see. "What are we going to do?"

"We?" Kent shook his head and held up his hands,

wishing he could block the words with them. "Not a chance in hell will I give you another damn cent. Remember when you didn't mind getting your hands dirty? You were side by side with me in the beginning. Maybe it's time you learn how to do things the hard way again, like the vast majority of everyone else in the world. Congrats though on making yourself destitute so quickly. Think it's a world record?"

"Don't be an asshole."

"Oh, oh, the irony of you telling me not to be an asshole." Kent risked a glance at the kitchen clock, not wanting Dusk to run into his ex-husband and misconstrue the situation. "You can go. I'm not your personal ATM. You've always been highly intelligent. Why don't you put it to good use?"

"Well," Spencer huffed.

"Well, what?"

Why had Spencer come? He'd been careful to keel all their joint accounts and property. What had he expected Kent to do for him?

"Don't you want to go back to how things were?" Spencer's voice had dropped down to the low, velvety tone which he'd always used to cajole Kent into things. He'd fallen for that voice in college. "We invested so many years together. Isn't it wrong to throw it all away without trying?"

Too little, too late, too forced.

All his angst about his inadequacies after the failure of his marriage came roaring back to Kent, an ugly reminder of the dark days right after his home had ceased to be his. He had contemplated going down on his knees to attempt to win his husband back. The love of his life. The man he'd expected to grow old with.

The laughter from Spencer and his new toy, William, echoed in his nightmares. Young Willie had been in his twenties, handsome, a football player turned model. Apparently, an athlete turned thief. Karma could indeed be quite a bitch.

"I've wanted to hear those words from your lips. I begged for them as I recall," Kent admitted. He could see the hope growing in those familiar onyx eyes. "The trouble is you broke our vows. The ones we fought so hard to have the right to make. You dragged me right into the sewer, left me there broken, bleeding, and alone. You tossed me aside with nothing. Not a damn thing to account for twenty plus years of my life but a ruined beach house in the Keys."

"Kent."

His heart clenched at the familiarity of how his name rolled off Spencer's tongue. "I can't. Not again.

You already threw away everything I had to give. How do you even have the nerve to ask for more?"

"We could try."

"Just get out." Kent couldn't handle another "we" out of the man's lying lips. His breath grew ragged while his breathing picked up along with his anger. "Get out of my home. Take your ass back to Colorado. Maybe your family will let you borrow a couch."

"Kent?"

Closing his eyes with a resigned groan, Kent waited for the impending fireworks. Spencer had obviously spotted the attractive shirtless man waltzing comfortably into the kitchen if his intake of breath were any indication. How could he not have? Dusk had a habit of standing out when he didn't even try.

"And who the hell are you?" Spencer had drawn himself up out of the chair. Kent didn't even have to open his eyes to know. He recognized the tenseness in his voice. "Well? Answer me? What are you doing in my husband's house?"

"Ex-husband, Spencer." Kent opened his eyes and decided to prevent the opening volley of World War III. "Meet Dusk, a local veterinarian."

"Dusk?" His former husband sneered the name. "Who names their kid that?"

"Mushrooms were involved," Dusk shrugged. He tossed a paper bag over to Kent. "Brought you donuts."

"Oh, how sweet." Spencer let the words fall off his tongue like liquid poison. "Does he deliver anything else? Or just donuts?"

"Bitter much?" Dusk hopped up on one of the kitchen counters, snagging Kent's coffee on the way. "I see why you weren't brokenhearted over him."

"Who the hell do you think you are?" Spencer started forward only to find Kent blocking his path. "I'm his husband."

"Ex-husband," Dusk interjected mildly. "I'm the man keeping the side of the bed that used to be yours warm. I'm the one giving him the best sex he's had in years. Who am I? His wet dream, your worst nightmare."

Kent couldn't help his snort of laughter. He struggled with imagining the laid-back hippie vet verbally eviscerating someone, yet he had. "Save me some coffee."

"Aren't you going to say something?" Spencer snapped at him.

Kent peered into the bag to grab one of the orange creamsicle ones before holding it out to him. "Want a donut?"

"We were married."

"Were." Kent set the bag on the table and his donut on top of it. "We *were* married. You didn't want to be anymore, so we aren't. It's all legal. I've even got the papers to prove it. I've nothing left for you."

"That's it?"

"Yep." Kent leaned against the table, trying to appear far more emotionally unattached than he was. "What did your grandmother always say? Don't let the door hit you where the good lord split you."

12

DUSK

GETTING IN THE MIDDLE OF FORMER LOVERS DIDN'T seem like a fun idea. Dusk almost wished his walk had taken longer. He had no place in this conversation, or even hearing it.

Conversation? More akin to a verbal walk across heated coals, nails, and broken glass. Kent certainly acted pained enough. His olive skin had an unhealthy ashen hue to it. His eyes were filled with so much anguish; Dusk couldn't stop from putting his opinion into the mix.

"Maybe you should take off?"

"I don't know what shack you crawled out of, but you can drag yourself back now." Spencer hadn't budged an inch, despite Kent trying to herd him outside. "Why should I leave?"

"Trespassing laws?" Dusk offered absently. He smirked behind his maple bacon donut when twin glares were aimed at him. "What? It's true. Did you invite him inside?"

"Technically? Yes," Kent grimaced. "I thought it was you. The invitation has been revoked."

"That only works on vampires." Dusk gestured to Spencer with the remaining chunk of his donut. "Open wide. Let's see those shiny teeth. Can you eat garlic?"

"Do you mind? This was a private conversation until you rudely cut in." Spencer's eyes narrowed on him before turning to his former spouse. "Couldn't we speak privately?"

"No." Kent caught his ex-husband by the arm to march him outside. "I'm done talking."

Leaving the divorcés to handle their business, Dusk stayed in the kitchen to make a pot of coffee to go with the donuts remaining in the bag. He studiously avoided eavesdropping on the raised voices coming from outside. *Don't need to know. I've no dog in the fight.*

Kent stormed inside after several loud, long minutes, rubbing his forehead vigorously with his fingers and muttering to himself. "I'm so sorry."

Dusk waved off the apology. "For what?"

"Forcing this train wreck of a morning on you?"

"Hurricane Spencer blew in with high winds, flooding of the mouth, and emotional destruction." Dusk earned a barely there smile for his attempt at a joke. "Maybe he's more of an earthquake or tidal wave?"

"Sinkhole." Kent collapsed into one of the newly painted and reupholstered chairs, accepting the fresh coffee handed to him with a grateful sigh. "We used to be so happy together."

"People who marry usually are."

"He's broke." Kent bent forward until his head rested on the table. "Broke. He squandered or simply lost two decades' worth of my legacy. And now? He has the balls to ask for more? He—"

"Screwed you over?"

The generally stoic, gray-haired builder broke off abruptly. Kent uttered one hoarse curse. It sounded as if it had been ripped forcefully from his gut. As Dusk watched him with growing concern, his shoulders started to tremble slightly. He punched the table once, covering up a heart-wrenching sob

Ahh, shit.

What am I doing?

His expertise in dealing with injured creatures tended toward those with four legs and fur—the odd bird and reptile as well. Human hurts, particularly the non-visible ones, were often significantly harder to heal. No amount of sweet treats or bad jokes would solve this one.

In his experience, the trouble with dealing with a broken heart started with rushing the process. If it took time to fall in love, why did people assume falling out of it happened in an instant? No matter the pain caused at the end, it couldn't magically erase everything which had come before.

"Donut?" Dusk, in hindsight, decided saying the first thing to pop into his head might not have been his greatest idea of the century. "Shot of whiskey? An entire bottle? I am the sole heir to a pub. Got spare keys and everything."

Kent choked on a sob, trying to force it into a laugh. "Thanks, but no. I think I'd prefer to be alone today if you don't mind. I'm not going to impress anyone in this mood."

"Alone? Nope. Terrible idea. Worst in the history of humanity, worse than buying tickets for the Titanic. Well, maybe not that bad." Dusk brushed the sticky glaze from the donut onto a napkin and balled it up to toss at the man's still bent head. "C'mon. Let's go."

"Where?" Kent surreptitiously wiped his eyes and

then lifted his head. "Not going on a dive today, too cold and windy."

"Annual wine tasting." Dusk had promised the owner of the wine shop to give them a hand setting things up for the event which started this year around noon. "We'll have lunch, get completely hammered on free booze, and this evening, we'll go around singing carols off-key and seeing all the Christmas lights. It's a tradition."

"What tradition?"

"Mine."

"It's not the *worst* plan ever." Kent rolled his shoulders slowly. He stretched his arms over his head, likely trying to release the tension in his muscles. "Not sure if I'm feeling festive enough."

"It'll keep you away from here if the sinkhole returns." He had to grin when Kent immediately disappeared into the bedroom. "Put on some jeans and bring a jacket with you. Cold air's blowing in from off the water. Damn December and its crazy weather fluctuations. It was perfect yesterday, now it's going to be cold tonight."

Rinsing the mug in the sink, Dusk pondered how best to approach the day. Kent had clearly been heavily affected by the sudden appearance of his ex-husband. He'd been shaken.

As sad as it was, the argument brought something to Dusk's attention. Did he want to play rebound for the at least partially damaged heart of the man in the other room? Did he even care either way?

Screwing around with each other, both aware of where they stood, it didn't seem overly risky. He might want to keep an eye on it. *And on myself.* He had no intentions of adding healing broken hearts to his job description.

"Fifty-eight degrees is *not* cold, you odd southerner."

"Not everyone lives in the mountains with snow, ice, and everything unpleasant." Dusk moved to stand in the doorway, watching Kent strip down to his boxers to change out of sweatpants into jeans. "You'll want a T-shirt, for now. It's in the sixties."

The day flew by in a flurry of tourists, locals, and glasses of wine. One of the popular food trucks had pulled up near Grand Vin for those wanting more than appetizers. They sat on a curb outside in the bright sunlight, eating Korean BBQ burritos and drinking wine.

So. Much. Wine.

As the sky grew darker and lights began to turn on, Dusk dragged Kent onto one of the Old Town Trolleys. He picked one filled with people he recognized.

He made sure to spike the cider they were handed with rum from a flask his dad had given to him earlier with a wink and a nudge.

The singing on their trolley became raucous almost immediately. They toured the island, looking at all the decorations, laughing with the others. Plates of cookies made the journey with them, though Tess and Hope had snuck food in as well. The married chef tossed Ziploc bags of more refined snacks down toward them, catching Dusk on the side of the head.

"Nice."

"Get your eat on, Dusky." Hope winked at him.

By the end of the night, the singing had become quite slurred and the songs almost unrecognizable. The two men giggled side by side with Hope and Tess when the trolley driver kicked them off on a corner. They joined another group of locals in Mallory Square, sharing cookies and hot Irish coffee.

They strolled through Mallory Square, down to the water's edge near the Schooner Wharf Bar, to catch the tail-end of the lighted boat parade. They sat on the sea wall, legs dangling above the water. Dusk thought, from the smile on Kent's face, that his mission to get his mind off the early morning drama had been a complete success.

Kent bumped his shoulder to get his attention. "Thanks."

"Walk down the beach to end the day?"

He shook his head. "Not yet."

The boats decked out in Christmas lights and decorations drifted by steadily. Music drifted over from the bar, mostly holiday-themed country songs. Dusk hummed along to some of them, allowing the cool air to wash over him amidst the warmth of the energy from the happy people around them.

"What are you doing on Christmas Day?"

Kent blinked in surprise, so lost in thought, the question took a moment to register. "I have traditions."

"Traditions?" Dusk found it his turn to be shocked. "You don't seem the type."

"I am." He didn't elaborate which made him incredibly curious. "What about you?"

"My parents refuse to celebrate." Dusk had wanted for nothing as a kid. His parents had gone above and beyond to provide for him, aside from meat and Christmas. On the whole, he'd never been deprived of anything and as an adult could do what he liked. "Mind company?"

As long as Mom doesn't know.

13
———
KENT

CHRISTMAS EVE LOOMED ON THE HORIZON. KENT HAD wrapped up the paperwork on selling the beach cottage, along with immediately using the funds to purchase two others. He would move out in January. The realtor had been excited to have a potential partner in the market and had many suggestions for future projects.

Kent wanted to survive December first. Make it through without committing homicide—or suicide. He had erroneously assumed Spencer would return to Colorado after his refusal to share funds.

I have never been so wrong in my entire life.

Each morning for the last eight days, Spencer had shown up at his door. He could almost admire his ex-husband's persistence. *Almost.* The begging had given way to arguing which had faded into shouting.

The latter had drawn the attention of the police. Spencer had been irate, assuming Kent or Dusk had called them. He couldn't get him to understand that standing outside screaming would definitely get the neighbors to respond.

The officer had been kind enough to simply give them a word of warning to calm things down and take them inside. Kent had been tempted to ask for an escort of Spencer off the property. He didn't think it would solve things.

I'm not petty enough to do it.

He also remembered the stark lesson from his high school coach to never invite the authorities into personal or family business unless absolutely necessary. *It's not their job to fix everyone's problems.* He'd never forgotten those words of wisdom.

"Kent?"

Not again.

Kent rolled out of bed, dragging himself toward the front of the house and the loud voice. He yanked the door to glare at Spencer. "What?"

"I'm going home. My flight leaves in a few hours." He gave a bittersweet smile. "You wouldn't believe me if I offered an apology for my behavior and I'm not sure I would mean it."

"Honesty, how refreshing."

"Yes," Spencer chuckled. "Will you ever forgive me?"

"Not enough to give you another dime." Kent had found with time his sadness over his broken marriage started to morph into a weary apathy. If anything, he only had a deep longing for peace. "I do wish you well. I hope you find whatever it is you're so eager to have."

"The district attorney has managed to track down William. Some of the money is being returned."

Oh, of course, Spencer doesn't actually need me anymore.

"Enjoy your life." Kent stepped inside and slammed the door shut. "Good riddance."

"Kent?" Spencer's voice was muffled by the wood. He knocked again. "Don't leave it like this, please?"

He reopened the door against his better judgement. "Well?"

Spencer held his hand out. "I doubt we'll be friends, but you were the love of my life for most of my life, at least until a few years ago. I won't spit on those memories by drawing this out any further. Be well, okay?"

Kent shook his hand with a tentative smile. "Stay away from wannabe models."

The door shut more gently this time around. The suspicious part of his mind wondered how much of that had been genuine. He just didn't know.

Damn.

Does it even matter?

Walking the short hallway out the back of the cottage, he sat on the steps of the deck with a weariness seeping into his bones. Hopefully, this would be the end of it with Spencer. He could honestly say he wished the man well.

There had been love at the start between them. Their relationship had been strong. They'd been well-matched.

Looking back on everything, Kent could see now how they had grown apart without realizing it. They'd been so young at the start and been through so many things together.

A painful life lesson perhaps on the scope of how relationships can go. No matter how much love there might be between two people, it wasn't always sufficient. When they married, no one had imagined it would fall apart.

Maybe that's part of it?We put so much into the fight for equality, we lost each other in the process.

In the months since their separation, Kent had spent much of it piling the blame onto Spencer. He couldn't help thinking it took two to tango. His narrow focus on work to the exclusion of everything else, his drive to earn more, do more, be more hadn't helped matters.

Could this be the catharsis for moving on?

Closure had always been missing from his divorce. They'd fractured so angrily, discourse had been done through attorneys. Now, though, they had managed to have some sort of conversation without shouting or insulting each other.

They'd been adults. They could let go. He could release the what-ifs from his mind.

"Deep thoughts for an almost Christmas Day."

Kent lifted his head to find his barefoot veterinarian had snuck up on him. *Mine? No, not mine, a barefoot veterinarian.* "No dogs?"

"The hotel is sadly canine free this week." Dusk plopped down onto the sand, knees bent up and hands resting behind him. "Saw your sinkhole heading down the street. You okay?"

"Yep, more than okay." Kent kicked sand at the man. "Don't call him a sinkhole."

"You're not getting back with him?" Dusk asked worriedly. "You can't be that senile, not yet."

"Oh, thanks." He sent another wave of sand at him. "No, he's decided to return to Colorado without me."

"Or your money?" Dusk threw in astutely. "He doesn't seem the type to give up easily."

"He isn't."

"Yet?"

Kent didn't quite know how to explain his gut instinct on it. "Closure."

"Good."

Okay, maybe I don't have to explain it.

"Are you wearing Santa shorts?" Kent tilted his head to the side to get a better view. "Merry Christmas Eve Eve?"

"You aren't nearly as grumpy as you were when I first met you," Dusk commented out of the blue.

"I ate the chickens."

"You didn't." Dusk shifted over to sit with his back against the older man's knees.

"Of course I didn't. I sleep with earplugs. It's done wonders for my mood." Kent barked out a laugh at the narrowed eyes glaring at him. "I speak the truth."

"Hmmph." He reached around to flick Kent on the inside of his knee. "You never did explain about your traditions."

Traditions?

"Christmas, you mean?"

At the enthusiastic nod, Kent pondered how best to explain his slightly odd way of celebrating this particular holiday. It had been something that had developed over time, starting as a child. Spencer had participated with him over the years, though not their last one together.

Stupid fool. How did I miss all the signs? Stop. Let it go. You've both moved on now. Damn stupid fool.

Growing up in a family that had considered Christmas to be a pagan festival, it hadn't been recognized *ever*. When his mother had told him about his father being not only Spanish but Catholic, a cardinal sin to their strict fundamentalist mindset, his curiosity had immediately been piqued. What had his dad believed? How would he have celebrated?

Without anyone aside from Kassandra knowing, Kent had started to research not only his heritage but his father's religion. He would never be a fierce defender of any faith. *Ever.* Yet, one time a year, it had become his way of honoring the man who he had never met.

He could still remember the joy of having his first tree. It had been tiny, almost Charlie Brown worthy. The puny thing had been hidden in the closet of his dorm room. No one ever saw it, other than Spencer who had a habit of celebrating any holiday with as much enthusiasm as possible.

His little sister, Kassandra, would send him a small present each year. Her way of showing her love went beyond her beliefs. She had always preferred to walk the talk, unlike the majority of their overly religious family.

"Do you go to mass?" Dusk broke the silence after his long trip down memory lane. "Advent candles and everything?"

His eyebrows rose up in surprise. "I do."

"I sneak into Saint Mary's to hear the carols," Dusk admitted. "The music is beautiful."

"Ahh." Kent had already researched the Christmas Mass times at The Basilica of Saint Mary Star of the Sea, the beautiful chapel in Key West. "I'm not Catholic."

"So?" He tilted his head back to grin up at Kent. "Don't have to be to enjoy the music or the season, do you? I'm down for blessings of any kind."

"Why am I not surprised?"

The two of them waved to the older couple who lived in the house to the left of his. Silence sank over them for a while. Kent could never quite get over how peaceful listening to the ocean could be.

His quiet time in Colorado, what rare moments of

it there had been, usually involved trips up to the mountains. Spencer enjoyed skiing and all things Aspen while Kent preferred camping out near Divide, and Mueller State Park, in particular, had become a personal favorite.

Kent couldn't remember the last time they had gone camping. Another sign of how deeply into becoming a workaholic he had gone. The more time passed, the more he thought over the last three years of their relationship, and it no longer surprised him they had separated.

Two to tango, indeed.

"Have a tree yet?"

"What?" Kent shook his head and focused on the man whose head was practically in his lap. His fingers came up to drift absently through the dirty-blond locks covering his knees. "Tree? Ahh, yes, I ran out of time."

"Want to go hunt for a tree?"

"Where?"

"Down the rabbit hole."

Kent stood up suddenly, causing Dusk to lose his balance. "How hard do you have to work to be this annoying?"

"Pure natural talent."

14

———

DUSK

The *Mission: Impossible* theme song rolled around in his head while he pondered where to find a Christmas tree on the twenty-third of December. The usual places had already sold out. Even the ones raising money for charity had none. *Now what?*

"I have an idea."

"Is it legal?" Kent pulled the truck up to a stop sign and side-eyed Dusk suspiciously. "Is it likely to increase my risk of death?"

"No." Dusk drew out the word with a mischevious grin. "Maybe? How attached are you to having something resembling a pine tree?"

"Not particularly attached."

They drove across the island—twice. Dusk lost count of the number of stores they'd checked out.

They'd found one set of trout lights which sounded as awful as they looked. One place had gotten them tinsel and flamingo ornaments but not a tree.

"Trout and flamingos." Kent twisted the box of Christmas lights around in his hand. "All I'm missing are a few beer cans and a palm tree."

"Could be worse."

"How?" Kent scratched his growing beard absently. "Where to next?"

"How do you feel about recycling?"

"Recycling?"

"Yep." Dusk recalled the stacks of boxes at the bar with empty bottles in them which would end up going to recycling in a couple of weeks. "Recycling."

Three hours later, Dusk added the final bottle to their tower of glass Christmas tree. They had draped the fish lights around it, dangling flamingos here and there to accent the true Key West vibe. He snapped a photo to show Jesse who would likely crack a rib laughing.

Kent stepped into the middle of the living room to survey their creation. He ran his fingers roughly through his gray hair. "Not sure this would be Church approved."

"Who doesn't approve of saving the planet?" Dusk popped the lid off one of the apple cider ales his dad had sent with them. He handed the second one to Kent. "Here's to a job well done."

Kent lifted the bottle in salute. "More like, here's to the most frat-worthy tree in the history of humanity."

Turning off the lights and closing the curtains to darken the room, Dusk dragged Kent over to the couch across from the tree. He flipped on the holiday lights, which cast a slightly nauseating pink and green hue over everything. A loud snort of laughter escaped before he could compress his lips together to stop it.

"Worse than I imagined." Kent clinked their bottle-necks together. "Merry Ho Ho Ho."

Dusk choked on a swig of his beer. "Think Santa will come through the window?"

"Maybe if we leave a beer out for him?" Kent grimaced after a second swig. "What is this shit?"

"Apple cider ale." Dusk brought the bottle up to get a closer look at the label. "Oh."

Kent frowned at him and used his phone to shed more light for them. "Apple cider with cherry? Who thought that was a good idea?"

The odd flavor combination might've worked in a pie, but not with the added bitterness of being turned into beer. They both set the drinks to the side almost in unison. He brought his hand up to wipe his tongue.

He twisted around on the couch to lie with his

head on Kent's muscular thigh, not the most comfortable of pillows. The fingers that dropped onto his head and combed through his hair made up for it. He almost drifted off to sleep in the dimly lit room, soothed by the gentle caresses.

"When do you have to move?"

Kent's fingers stilled briefly before continuing their stroking. "January. I made it part of the contract. Moving over the last two weeks of the year would've been a nightmare, even if everything I own fits in my truck. I'll start renovations on the two cottages on the third or fourth."

"No returning to Colorado?"

"Nothing there for me." Kent eased his leg out from under Dusk's head and got to his feet. He flipped the lights on and reopened the curtains. "What about you? What are your plans for the clinic?"

"I've got enough money saved up now to purchase most of the supplies, but not to cover labor." Dusk had spent hours earlier in the week with his dad going over all the numbers. He'd hoped to hire contractors at the start of the year, but decided to do some of the easier tasks like drywall and floors himself. His work with Kent on the cottage had given him at least a bit of a foundation for how to manage it. "It's probably going to take until the summer to be up to normal function. Not how I wanted, but certainly better than other businesses who had to pack up and leave."

"Can I help?"

"You know how to swing a hammer." He wouldn't turn down an extra set of hands who knew what they were doing. "Jesse promised to help with putting in drywall, but he'll spend most of the time drinking and harassing me to fix his spots."

Kent opened his mouth to respond only to pause when someone began knocking. "Damn. Maybe they'll go away?"

"Not your ex is it?"

"God, I hope not, he's supposedly already on a plane by now." Kent wandered toward the front door with Dusk close on his heels, too nosy to stay put on the couch. He opened up and froze, staring at the balding man on his stoop. "Can I help you?"

"I am Ramon Casado." He had a hint of an accent, which Dusk thought might be Spanish and on closer inspection looked remarkably like Kent. "Your mother gave me this address for you."

Kent stared blankly at him, not moving or speaking for several awkward seconds. "She did. Of course she did, and didn't bother to tell me."

"You broke your phone," Dusk interjected helpfully. He caught Kent by the arm to guide him inside, calling over his shoulder for *Ramon Casado* to follow. "Maybe more ale?"

"Because being even more nauseated would help how?" Kent grimaced at him. He shook his head and seemed to center himself, turning toward his father who stood proudly though uneasily in the living room. He stuck his hand out toward the man. "I'm Kent Casado, your son."

15

KENT

ON HIS MENTAL LIST OF PEOPLE WHO MIGHT HAUNT HIS door, Ramon Casado had definitely not even come close to the top ten names, or hundred for that matter. *Maybe I shouldn't have ignored all those emails?* Regrets would have to wait until after this life-altering moment had finished.

"Interesting decorations." His father's—His. Father. —eyes roamed around the room, curiously stopping on the stack of amber bottles in the corner. "This was done on purpose?"

"Options were limited." Kent had no idea how to handle himself. The world appeared to be going in fast forward while his mind functioned in slow motion. "Did you have a long trip?"

Oh. My. God. This is so awkward I am having an out of body experience.

"Around four hours. I drove down from Miami. I own Casado & Associates, an architecture firm. I started it in my hometown of Sevilla before moving to Miami fifteen years ago." Ramon eased down into the armchair which Dusk directed him toward when Kent showed no signs of regaining his ability to speak more than inane inquiries. "I always hoped to one day meet you. She only told me after you had become a teenager."

"Why now?" Kent's knees finally gave, and he dropped onto the sofa. Dusk squeezed his shoulder and muttered about going to find something for dinner, making a discreet exit and leaving father and son alone. "Why wait until now? I'm in my forties."

"Your mother made it quite clear my presence would be unwelcome by her, her family, and by you. She made it sound almost as if I had abandoned the both of you." He gesticulated eloquently with his hands, speaking with them nearly as much as with his words. "How could I when I knew nothing about you? We met in our late teens when she was vacationing in Madrid, and shared a few days and nights together. I knew nothing else until a letter arrived after your fourteenth birthday. Another showed up not long after your graduation from college. I have no other children, only you."

Kent struggled with understanding what the man had claimed, an all too believable shift in the story his mother had told him of his conception and the circumstances involving his father's mysterious absence in his life. "You wanted me?"

His father's eyes, so identical in color to his own, filled with unshed tears. "*Claro que si.* Yes, yes, of course. Always, from the second I knew I had a son—a son. I wanted to be in your life, to show you how to be a good man, a strong one. Now, though, you've grown past the years where you need a father's help."

"I did." He choked on the rest of the words he longed to share with the man. "I dreamed about you so often. Every birthday, I wished for you. Prayed for you every Sunday. God never answered."

Ramon sat forward with his fingers twitching as if to reach out before aborting the move, his hands gripping the arms of the chair instead. "I didn't want to intrude."

"I'm all grown up."

"Would you allow me the honor of getting to know you?" His emotions were hard to read, but his body language reeked of expecting to be rejected altogether. "I'm here for the holiday. Do you celebrate? Your mother never did. I remember her ranting about my heathen ways."

Kent found it impossible to speak. Here in the form of a man in his sixties was the answer to all of his birthday wishes to spend time with his dad. *Say something, idiot.* "Yes."

Oh great, I'm sure that cleared things up for him.

"Yes?"

"I celebrate Christmas." He fought a blush for the first time in maybe twenty-five years. "For you. Mom said you were Catholic. Not sure I ever managed to accurately portray how you might've spent Advent, but I tried. I used to pretend you were there with me, lighting the candles and listening to the music."

"Do you attend Mass?" Ramon asked eagerly, likely wanting every bit of information about his child offered.

"Only on Christmas." Kent hesitated briefly but decided not to hide who he was from anyone. "I'm gay."

His father returned his gaze without reaction. "If *El Papa* refuses to judge, who am I to do so? I need only know one thing about you—you are my son."

Better than instant condemnation. Not sure I could've handled both of my parents insisting I'm hell bound.

"Will you tell me about the Casados?" Kent had wondered for most of his life.

Who were they? Where did they come from? Did any of their traits get passed down? Questions he thought most children wondered if they had never known their family.

Over the course of severals hours, two pots of coffee, and some ginger cookies Dusk had brought over, Kent learned about his family. Ramon had been the son and grandson of a builder. The Casados had a long history in construction and masonry.

They shared a laugh at how Kent had continued in the family business without even knowing. It had been in his blood. Strength also ran in the Casados; his father told stories of his grandfather who had supported his mother and siblings when Ramon's great-grandfather had passed away.

Pulling out his wallet, Ramon showed a handful of tiny photos. *His mother, his brother, his sister, nephews, and nieces.* Kent's emotions spilled over at having finally connected the two halves of his soul. He learned something new then. His father gave powerful and encompassing hugs.

As the biracial son of a biracial mother, Kent had grown up frequently teased by his peers. Never quite fitting into the non-mixed members of the maternal side of his family on either the Caucasian or African-American sides. He had the added distinction of having claims to Spanish ancestry.

His grandfather on his mother's side had shared stories of his great grandmother who had come from Finland and her husband who had been the captain of a ship from the Ivory Coast. No one knew how they'd met or arrived in America, some stories lost to time apparently. The Edwards family had been proud of their lineage, what they knew of it.

Kent had always wanted to hear more about the Casados. *Now I know.* He wrapped his arms firmly around his father. *"Thank you."*

Thank you.

Two words had never been quite so inadequate. They returned to their separate seats around the kitchen table, hiding behind coffee mugs. Uneasy, but not quite ashamed of their expression of love.

"You'll stay, right? For Christmas and New Year's?" Kent didn't know whether they could build a father-son connection, certainly not over the course of a week, but a foundation could be made. "Dusk promised a meal, you could join us."

"Dusk? Your boyfriend?"

"No, friend." Kent's instinctual and immediate

response earned a laugh out of his father, and an "are you sure?" and he was—certain. "Only a friend."

"Hmm." Ramon slowly stirred his coffee, clicking the spoon against the sides. "My Caterina laughed at me the way you laughed at your friend when I began to first court her. Love came much later."

"Caterina? Your wife?"

"*Si*," Ramon nodded. "We've been married for over thirty years. She stayed in Miami, long drives are hard on her."

"No children?"

He shook his head sadly. "We tried, but couldn't. She encouraged me to reach out to you before life got too much further away from us."

"I'm glad."

"Are you?"

Kent caught his father's hand in his own, squeezing the rough hands so similar to his own tightly. "I am. Best present I could have ever imagined receiving this Christmas."

He meant it. In all those years of hoping, deep in his heart, he had never believed it would happen. Now it had. Proof he had a father, one who wanted him and cared to be in his life.

I am too old to be this damn happy.

For the first time in his life, Kent would be able to

attend a service at church with his father. The man who had inspired his attending every year on the twenty-fourth of December. It meant this might go from the worst year of his life to the best.

"Knock, knock?"

Kent threw a cookie at Dusk who had waltzed into the house without *actually* knocking. "Might've been more useful if you had done that to the door."

"I assumed four hours would be enough time for you to get the tears out of the way." The blond waved the bag again. "I brought burgers and fries."

"I should return to my hotel." Ramon started to stand only for Dusk to rest a hand on his shoulders. His eyes held obvious and unfettered hope. "I shouldn't return?"

"I got enough for the three of us." Dusk set the food down in the center of the table and made himself at home in the kitchen by getting drinks, paper plates, and napkins. He froze when he spotted Kent staring at him intently. "What?"

"Nothing."

With his father's comments about his wife ringing in his ears, Kent observed Dusk in a completely new light. He figured they had both been working under the same assumptions about this being the most casual of casual relationships. All sex, no muss or fuss about emotions or anything else to complicate their lives unnecessarily.

Perfect, right?

Yet, here the man danced around Kent's kitchen, perfectly at ease. Dusk shimmied by the fridge, grabbing a selection of beers and sodas, carefully balancing them in his hands to place on the table. Ramon sent his son a knowing smile, which he chose to disregard.

It struck him as odd how Dusk had been there for two of his roughest emotional experiences ever. The barefoot hippie had offered more comfort and support than his family through the painful closure with Spencer. He had also now gone out of his way to ease the first meeting between father and son.

Who does all of that for a man they've only known for a few months? Is he this kind to everyone? Or, is Ramon right? Ramon—should I call him dad, father, papa? I am too damn old for this.

"To breaking bread for the first time." Ramon lifted his soda in salute to both of them. "May this be a joyous season."

While eating together, Dusk, in his typically laid-back manner, asked unobtrusive questions. He put all three of them at ease. The awkwardness faded away as they continued to share stories and facts about their lives.

Kent reached underneath the table to squeeze Dusk's knee with a grateful smile. He turned to find his father once again watching them intently. "Have you seen much of the island?"

"I came straight here upon arriving. I have booked a room at a hotel, but haven't yet checked in or explored the Keys. It's my first time here." Ramon wiped his fingers on a napkin Dusk handed to him. "Perhaps you two could show me the sights? I understand they take special care with lights and decorations at this time of year."

"Trolley time?" Dusk broke into a broad smile. He pulled out his phone and scrolled through numbers. "I could call in a favor for a personal tour. Who doesn't enjoy Christmas lights?"

"Can you handle an evening ride around the Keys on a tram?" Kent didn't think the owner of the trolley would be quite so willing to offer services after they'd gotten kicked off the thing a few days ago. Dusk could certainly be charm personified when he wanted. His father shrugged, only seeming to care that he could spend time with his son. "No spiked eggnog this time."

"Spoilsport." Dusk crossed his arms, struggling rather unsuccessfully to turn his grin into a pout.

16

————

DUSK

The week between Christmas and New Year's did not go as expected. Dusk spent time with his parents and also watched the blossoming relationship between the Casado men. It had been painfully sweet in the Hallmark movie, touchy-feely, and warm fuzzies kind of way.

Sitting on the stairs in his gutted clinic early on January first, Dusk considered all the emotionally heavy moments in Kent's life, which he had witnessed. Things one would expect to share with family or a longtime lover, not a new fling. How had they gotten so entangled?

He liked Kent. Hot, intelligent, capable, and built like a brick wall. What wasn't there to enjoy? Enjoying themselves didn't mean anything deeper as far as emotions went, hadn't in the past. They both understood the nature of the game and felt free to casually indulge with each other.

The end of the year struck him more intensely for some reason. Instead of enjoying the revelry at the Barefoot Saloon, Dusk snuck off to hermit away in his clinic and think about the past, future, and inevitably, Kent. A man who continued to bewilder his expectations of how his only sexual relationships usually went.

"Dusk? You in here?"

Dusk brought his hand up to shield his eyes from the sudden brightness of a flashlight being swung in his direction. "Derrick?"

"Got a call about an intruder at the clinic." Derrick Walker had been in Key West as long as Dusk. His parents had moved to the island a few years after the Walkers. They'd grown up together, close friends and confidants. "I thought you'd been spending the nights at your folks' place over the holidays? What're you doing out here at three in the morning on New Years? You all right?"

"Fit as a fiddle."

Derrick crouched at the foot of the stairs, putting himself at eye level with Dusk. "You'll get this place up and running again soon."

"I know."

"You should get some sleep, Dusk. You've never done well without a good eight hours." Derrick had worked a paper route with him when they were in their teens. He'd often required being dragged out of bed in the early hours of the morning. "Want a ride to the bar?"

"Remember Hurricane Irene in '99 when we were fourteen?" Dusk's question caught his old buddy by surprise. Derrick stood up and then squashed in next to him on the stairs to sit. "We thought we could ride it out on our own, snuck out in the middle of it. Or Hurricane Andrew?"

"I have nightmares about Andrew. We lost the roof of our house." Derrick shuddered dramatically. "Why do you ask?"

"Old Mrs. Wilson."

"Ahh." Derrick rubbed tiredly at his eyes, setting his flashlight on the stairs between his legs. "I heard her funeral was last week. She wouldn't evacuate because her husband was in the hospital after a heart surgery."

The Wilsons had lived in Key West for longer than Dusk could remember. They had been in their nineties when they passed away. He had crystal clear memories of the terrifying moment during Hurricane Andrew when they'd had to rescue her and her two dogs from floating away in the storm surge. They'd been scared out of their minds, helping their fathers save lives.

"Made me want to become a police officer." Derrick had become obsessed with law enforcement not long after, volunteering his free time all the way through high school to the police department, anything to get closer to his goal of officer. "Why bring all this up now?"

"How many times will I end up rebuilding this place? Old Man Wilson said they lost their home what, five or six times?" Dusk had been pushing so hard for his clinic, refusing help; he didn't know how much he had left. Kent had provided such an incredibly attractive distraction. "Ignore me, I'm tired."

"Let's get you home. Your mom'll be madder than that time I let you get all sunburnt, and she tried to drown you in a milk bath to soothe the pain." Derrick's laugh boomed out into the darkness. Big laugh for a big man, six foot eight, bright honey eyes, and rich umber skin inherited from his proudly Haitian parents. He'd been the wet dream of most of the girls *and* some of the boys in high school. "Stop ogling me in my uniform. We tried, remember?"

"Try is a generous term for one make-out session where you ended up breaking my nose in your enthusiasm." Dusk easily dodged the elbow sent his way. "Truth hurts, doesn't it?"

"I distinctly recall it being your own damn fault you broke your nose and not mine." Derrick attempted to blind him with the flashlight again. "C'mon, I'll give you a lift. You need a nap."

"Yes, Officer Walker."

"Idiot. Your dad is probably waiting up for you."

"Yep."

Fuck-a-doodle-do.

His dad was waiting up for him, on the porch with Jesse. They lifted glasses of sweet tea at the younger men. "Officer Derrick, last time you two snuck in this late, I had to explain why six chickens had been snuck into the post office."

"His idea." Dusk immediately pointed toward Derrick. "All him."

"Hey! I'm all about law and order."

"Maybe you are now." Dusk snickered unrepentantly at his taller friend. "Don't you have a patrol to do? Wait, why are you doing patrol, anyway? Thought you'd been promoted?"

"Volunteered." Derrick shoved him toward the house. "If you're done being funny, get your ass into bed. Oh, by the way, my mom wants you to bring the

Colorado man over for dinner next week so we can all meet him."

"She *what?*"

The traitor ignored his horrified gasp and hopped into his squad car with a cheerful wave. He drove off without another word. *Great.* He blinked tiredly at the smiling men on the porch and trudged by them into the house without another word, suddenly too exhausted to deal with old gossips.

For not having gotten drunk, Dusk woke up with a hell of a hangover. He stumbled into the kitchen to find his parents with equally disturbing smiles on their faces. Their laughter followed him when he made a sharp turn to head out of the house.

His morning required something other than a vegan muffin. Coffee, lots of coffee, maybe an overdose of sugar from Glazed Donuts on Eaton Street, might jump start his brain. He hoped Derrick wasn't still doing his rounds; his swerving on his bicycle would draw unwarranted attention.

Coffee in hand, Dusk fell on his three donuts, inhaling them without any remorse. He licked the sticky sugar from his fingers and gulped down his cooling nectar of the heavens. *Ahh, awake. Happy 2017 to me. What am I going to do this year?* The funds in his bank account would cover a large number of the supplies required to fix at least part of the clinic.

I can do this.

"Save one of those for me?" Jesse dropped down beside him on the curb. "Can't you sit on benches or chairs like normal folk?"

"Nope." He held out the empty bag. "Nope to both of your questions."

"I sat down for this?" Jesse shook out the few flakes of glaze onto the ground. "Son of a…"

"You have met my mother."

"Terrifyingly kind woman."

He wasn't wrong.

"Colorado Man's father left this morning. You should go see him." Jesse crumpled up the bag and flung it at Dusk. "Bring him breakfast, if you can manage not to eat it on the way."

"Shit. Are you the one spreading the gossip about him and me?"

"Who, me? Old Jesse never gossiped about no one." He heaped on a thick southern drawl. "You have spent weeks and weeks working on the man's house with him."

"Weeks and weeks?"

"Yep." Jesse's grin refused to be dimmed no matter how much Dusk frowned at him. "Is that Ms. Alice?"

"And, I'm gone."

Bolting to his bicycle, Dusk made a quick escape to avoid getting his behind pinched. Maybe he could check in on Kent. The man would be packing up to move into one of his new houses so he might need a hand.

Oh shit. I am so in lust.

He shrugged mentally, not bothered by a bit of infatuation. Crushing on a man at least ten years his senior didn't faze him at all. He saw no point in letting other people's issues become his own.

After swinging by to grab breakfast tacos, Dusk cycled through the mostly empty streets to reach Kent's beach house. From the few boxes and bags in the bed of the truck, the moving process had already begun. He leaned his bike against the palm tree in the yard and headed inside.

"I come bearing gifts." Dusk found the object of his infatuation prone on the kitchen floor with his head and shoulders hidden inside the cabinet underneath the sink. "Got a leak?"

Kent sat up, banging his head against the pipe if the clang he heard meant anything. "Shit."

"Hungry?"

He slid out from the cabinet with a hand rubbing a

red spot on his forehead. "A little warning would've been nice."

"I said I came bearing gifts." Dusk perched on the counter and pulled out a taco to offer to him. "What's the issue?"

"Changing out the pipes on all the sinks per the realtor's request, last thing I have to do before I leave." Kent sniffed the food appreciatively. "No coffee?"

"Drank it."

"Damn." He sank onto one of the chairs while making quick work of scarfing down several of the tacos. He peered at Dusk with a disturbing intensity. "You sleep at all last night? I could pack the entire house in the bags under your eyes."

Dusk snorted and yanked the food bag out of reach. "No more tacos for you."

"Full anyway."

Dusk stuck his tongue out at him. "I may have had an exceptionally late night and an incredibly early morning."

"Those adjectives were completely unnecessary." Kent grabbed a Styrofoam cup from the counter, shaking it gently. "Shit. No coffee. I've finished up here. Are you coming with me to help me unload the truck?"

"My tired eyes might not be able to handle it." Dusk

collapsed dramatically on the kitchen counter before falling off when Kent shoved him. "Do you want help or not?"

"Should I point out you were the one to come over without invitation?" He disappeared into the bedroom and living room, likely checking for anything he'd missed. "Ready?"

Getting up off the floor, Dusk gathered up the bag and wrappers from breakfast to throw away in the large garbage cans outside. He followed Kent out, watching him lock up the house. His bicycle got stowed in the back of the truck while they went inside.

"Coffee first?"

"Always." Dusk rolled the window down and leaned his head partially out of it to enjoy the ocean breeze. "Did your dad take off?"

"This morning." Kent spared a glance at him. "You okay? You seem—off."

"Off?"

"Yeah, off." He shifted the truck into gear. His attention split between the road and frowning at Dusk. "Something happen last night?"

Dusk twisted his head to stare at himself in the side mirror. "I don't *feel* off. Maybe it's 'cause I didn't get enough sleep."

Closing his eyes against the brilliant January sun,

Dusk allowed the rushing air to fling his hair every which way. He didn't know what Kent had seen to concern him. Nothing seemed off within himself, not that he'd noticed.

"New Year funk?"

"*Dude*. Dude, let it go. I'm fine, no funk to be had." Dusk brought his head back inside the truck and rolled the window up. "How many rooms in this cottage?"

"Two bedrooms."

"How many rooms can we christen today?" Dusk dropped his hand on Kent's jean-covered thigh, massaging the taut muscles. "I think we can get the kitchen and bedrooms at the very least, maybe the bathroom as well."

The first house on Kent's renovation list turned out to be an old beach rental, which had been used by college kids during the summer season. It had been empty ever since and was in need of a clean out and a fix up. Dusk hoped all the house flipping would bring more people who wanted to stay in the Keys to live, like his parents, and not simply vacation for a few months out of the year.

Older than the previous one, Dusk had the distinct impression this would require more effort from Kent. He'd be stuck in the Keys longer if both his newly bought properties were the same. *Good.* He enjoyed the sex and the company too much to wish him gone too soon.

Unloading the truck took a relatively short amount of time. A few boxes, bags, and construction supplies, plus all the groceries which had been brought over immediately went into the fridge. Beer, a massive priority for any Key West resident, had an entire shelf to itself.

A beer.

Fucking.

The ocean.

The best things in the world outside of family and healing animals, in my humble opinion.

"Two."

Dusk dragged his eyes away from looking out the window toward the beach to find Kent watching him with an assessing gleam in his eyes. "Two what?"

"Number of rooms we can christen." Kent grabbed the hem of his shirt to rip it over his head, revealing his defined abs. "Maybe three, if you're up for it."

"Always."

17

———

KENT

They started in the hallway.

Clothes were strewn from the front door, down toward the kitchen where they'd hunted for the condoms and lube. Boxes and bags had been opened until the desired objects were located underneath a can of coffee in one of the containers with the food. Kent tossed them onto a counter and grinned hungrily at the naked man in front of him.

One hand caught Dusk by the shoulder to drag him closer. Kent spun him around within his arms. His fingers skated up his sides to pause at his nipples, dancing circles around the stiffening nubs, eliciting an instant moan, and arching the back of his willing captive.

His tongue swirled around the edge of Dusk's ear

before exploring the side of his neck, nibbling at the underside of his jaw. Kent smirked against his jaw when a hand dropped over his and forcefully guided both down his stomach to drift into the bright blue briefs, the only article of clothing either of them still wore, and wrapped their joined fingers around his arousal.

"Eager, are we?" Kent teased with a swipe of his tongue along the outer shell of his lover's ear. He chuckled wickedly at the bucking body in his arms. "So sensitive, so desperate for more."

They stroked the hard shaft together. Dusk twisted his head around to the side until their lips could meet. They groaned into each other's mouths when Kent rubbed himself against the toned, rounded rear in front of him.

Kent tugged his fingers free, resting both of his hands on Dusk's shoulders to turn him and gently guide him to his knees. He bumped his shaft against that kiss-swollen mouth. "Suck."

Dusk peered up at him with a sly smile. "Resorting to one-word demands?"

He jutted his hips forward to lightly smack against the slightly parted lips. "Why write a novel when a sentence will do? Suck, damn it."

With one hand going around to splay across Kent's

behind, Dusk had apparently decided to throw teasing out the window. His tongue whisked over his sensitive head ever so briefly before engulfing his arousal in the wonderfully wet and warm heat of his mouth.

Kent's fingers tangled roughly in the tousled blond hair of the man to pull him off. "Get up here. Changed my damn mind."

Yanking him into a kiss, Kent wanted to possess the man through the voracious caress. His tongue bumped against the jewelry in Dusk's mouth, which as always sent a shudder down his spine straight to his dick. He groaned into his mouth, voice dropping to a gravelly depth.

Reaching blindly behind him for the lube left on the counter, Kent tossed the small bottle to Dusk with a pointed glare. The younger man smirked at him before making a lewd meal out of slicking his fingers to prepare himself. He found it almost impossible to look away or even start to open the condom wrapper, earning himself a dark chuckle.

Preparation complete, Kent pushed Dusk up against the cold steel of the refrigerator. He laughed at the hiss from the man whose nipples had come into contact with the coolness. One slow roll of his hips and his shaft sank deep into that glorious tight heat.

For the rush of their foreplay and preparation,

Kent had an unshakeable need to take his time. His measured thrusts dragged groans of complaint from Dusk, but he maintained his unhurried pace. Minutes went by until their bodies shook with the overwhelming urge to crest into blissful pleasure, sweat dripping from his nose down his partner's spine.

"Can't. *Have to*," Dusk gasped out.

"*Fuck.*" Kent found it impossible not to follow when the tightness clamped down around his shaft, forcing his climax. He dropped his forehead against the back of Dusk's neck with one arm around the man and his other hand gripping desperately for the door of the fridge to keep them on their feet. "God. Damn. So damn good."

Dusk breathed heavily in his arms, knees almost going out from under him. "One down? Where next?"

"Hang on."

The trail of clothing might've led from the front door to the kitchen, but it was condoms and foil wrappers playing breadcrumbs from the fridge, down the hall, into the living room, and through to the master bedroom. They christened three of the main spaces in the house before collapsing on their backs, spent, on the uncovered mattress with equally exhausted sighs of contentment.

Too tired to do much of anything, Kent barely

knew what was happening until Dusk had stroked him to hardness. A condom quickly slid down on his arousal. The younger man who had way more energy than was normal threw his leg over the prone contractor and slid himself down onto his shaft.

A hand sought his, knotting their fingers together, while Dusk rode him to yet another orgasm, the slowest and hardest of the day to achieve. He hadn't believed either of them had one left. He was definitely mistaken.

So damn wrong.

The tanned, muscled body of the man currently screwing himself on his dick became a mesmerizing sight. Kent wondered if he'd been hypnotized by it. He couldn't bring himself to do much more than reach between them and casually stroke Dusk's own arousal, fingers curled around to allow it to slide in and out each time the man lifted up and down.

And then, finally.

They were both spent, physically and sexually. Kent glanced toward the bathroom door, but couldn't find the energy to drag himself into the room to clean up. Dusk tossed the last of their condoms in the general direction of the trash can in the corner and dropped onto the bed with a tired grunt.

"We should clean up."

"Right," Dusk mumbled, already sounding half asleep.

"We'll be crusty if we don't."

"Right."

Napping hadn't been part of his plan for the day, but they slept for several hours. Waking up with the evidence of their christening marathon dried on his stomach had him cringing.

Dusk's eyelids fluttered before opening fully. He stretched his arms and legs out before regretting it almost immediately. "Oh, ow. Why did I decide that last time was a good idea?"

"No idea."

"I'm crusty."

"Told you." Kent grunted when an arm flopped onto his stomach. "Shower?"

Dusk nodded so minimally he almost missed it. "Fuck-a-doodle-do."

"Just realized you weren't in your early twenties anymore?"

"Yeah." Dusk flopped over on his side and grinned at him. "I'm consoling myself in the knowledge that at least I'm not in my forties."

Deciding to respond like the mature adult, Kent shoved the idiot off the side of the bed. Dusk landed on the floor in a tangle of his limbs. He stood with a sniff, his only answer to being rolled off the mattress, and made his way into the bathroom.

"Got any towels?"

Kent grabbed his toiletry bag and towels before joining the veterinarian in the shower. He hissed in surprise when ice cold water hit his back. "You couldn't have turned on the hot?"

"Revenge is a dish best served cold."

They showered quickly once the water warmed up a little. Their shafts gave kicks of interest at the soapy, roaming fingers. Neither of them could manage more than a halfhearted hint of arousal.

Too much sex, not enough sleep.

His stomach growled loudly.

Or food.

Padding through the house barefoot with a towel around his waist, Kent retrieved their clothing. He laughed when he had to stand on his tip toes to grab the socks that had found their way up on top of the cabinets. *How the hell did they get up there?*

"Found your trousers on the fan. I don't remember us sending them in that direction." Dusk wandered into the kitchen to join him. He rubbed his fingers across his stomach, the move stretching the veterinarian symbol tattoo on his forearm. "So, I think we should indulge our sex-comas with pizza, affogatos, and maybe a pint or four of gelato?"

"Affogato?"

"Think an espresso milkshake with scoops of gelato," Dusk said dreamily.

"Is that legal?" Kent had to laugh when they tossed their clothing back and forth when he realized the briefs in his hand belonged to Dusk who had a hold of his boxers. "We certainly worked up enough of an appetite."

"We did—shit." Dusk's foot skidded out from under him when he stepped on a condom. "I haven't slipped on a used condom since college."

After picking up an oven-baked meatball pizza and their espresso floats from Duetto's, Dusk guided him to one of the nearby marinas. They sat on the seawall outside of the *members* only cordoned off area, legs dangling over the edge, the box of food between them. One sip of the drink told him that they'd both be wired for hours.

Strong ass espresso.

The breeze off the water made it the perfect winter's day in Key West. They ate their way through the medium pizza, replenishing the calories they'd burned through during their sensual marathon. Kent thought he might've gained two pounds from the affogato alone, never mind the addictive pie with its mounds of meatballs, rich cheese, and sauce.

Kent wiped his greasy fingers on a napkin and snorted at the loud belch from the man to his left. "Classy."

"Some consider it rude not to burp after a meal."

"Frat boys don't count."

"No, seriously, I think it's in Thailand where they get all up in arms if you don't let one rip after a meal." Dusk waved his cup around, taking a sip and pointing it at Kent. "You mock, but I'm pretty sure it's true."

"Have any plans for the day?" Kent had intended to make a start on the renovations, but the sex and the food brought on a lazy fog. "Working on your clinic?"

"Next week." He tilted his head back when the sun broke through the clouds. "Best time of the year, right now. Sunny but cool enough not to melt you into the sidewalk."

"Why next week?"

"Jesse and Derrick promised to give me a hand with the second floor of the clinic. It had the most damage. The structural stuff's all fixed up, but it needs floors and shit before I can move in full time and stop sleeping at my parents' place." Dusk grabbed the empty box and napkins, hopping off the seawall to toss it all in a nearby trash can. "Dad would help, but his back's still jacked up."

"Want me to…"

"You have your houses to flip." Dusk shook his head abruptly, sending his mop of hair flying around. "I'll get it done."

"Are you…"

"I'll get it done."

Okay, then.

18

———

DUSK

February

ON ONE OF THE RARE COOL MORNINGS OF A KEY WEST winter, Dusk stood staring blankly at the white truck parked outside of his clinic. He didn't recognize the construction company logo on the side of the vehicle and definitely hadn't contacted them. Three workers climbed out and eyed him expectantly.

"Can I help you?" Dusk realized they had intended to park in front of his clinic when they started unloading their gear. "Are you lost? Don't think anyone around here has work going aside from me. I certainly couldn't have afforded to hire you unless I've gotten a sudden case of amnesia."

"Dusk Keller, right?" One of the workers peered at

the clipboard in his hand. "Got your name here, says we're supposed to help with fixing up your vet hospital."

"I didn't hire you." Dusk could only gawk dumbly at the work order handed to him. "I mean, I'd remember doing it, pretty confident I wouldn't have forgotten forking over that much cash."

"Old buddy of our boss from the Midwest called last week. Castro? Castano? Centeno? Casado! That's the one." He turned to gesture to the rest of the crew to finish unloading. "He said he'd join us later. So, where we starting?"

"Starting?" Dusk held both hands up to attempt to stop all movement while trying to process what he was being told. "I didn't hire you."

"Yes, it's a gift," he spoke slowly. "A gift."

Dusk spun around to compose himself, hands shoved into the pockets of his jeans. He counted backward from ten—three times. His breathing evened out enough for him to turn and speak like a faintly intelligent human being. "Two blocks east, first house on the left, there's a single father with four kids. Lost his wife to cancer. He can't afford to fix his home up. Tell him an anonymous benefactor donated your time to him."

"Mr. Keller."

"Don't you want to help a deserving family down

on their luck?" Dusk kept his cool, barely. He reminded himself repeatedly not to blame the messenger. They had no idea how vehemently he had argued against having his way paid for him. "Well? Go on, get. I'm serious."

The three-man crew, well two men and a woman, exchanged glances before shrugging, returning to their vehicle, and taking off. Dusk hoped they would help Raj and his kids. They'd moved down from Miami a few years ago to run a curry food truck near Mallory Square. He ate there once a week.

Best damn curry in Florida.

To channel his anger, he threw himself into installing the new linoleum floors, which would cover the exam room, surgery, and receptionist area. He had already finished with the treated concrete for the small kennel in the rear of the clinic, and the upstairs apartment had a lovely wooden floor he'd gotten cheap from a close-out sale.

January was spent getting the upstairs finished. He'd moved back in at the end of the month, much to his mom's disappointment and his joy. His parents were amazing people, but no one in their thirties really wanted to be living at home.

His goal for February was to get all the flooring done. One section of the surgery room had already been finished with Jesse's help. The repairs were on track to be completed before the beginning of summer.

Thank God.

The object of his ire made his appearance late in the morning. Kent brought coffee from Starbucks. He set the cups on the hood of his truck and glanced around bewildered.

"Expecting someone?" Dusk patted himself mentally on the back for managing to sound unbothered. "Or, several someones?"

Kent crossed his arms and rested against the truck. "I'm guessing the contractors showed up this morning."

"They did."

"And?"

"I recommended they go to my neighbor's a few blocks away who can use the extra hands." Dusk returned his own hands to his pockets, safest way to avoid doing something idiotic. "Why?"

"I wanted to help." He seemed completely oblivious to why Dusk might be upset. "You are familiar with the concept, right? Help? I can provide the definition."

"You want to *help* me? Bring your hammer, not your credit card." Dusk yanked on his hair, shoving the wavy strands out of his face. "How many times did

I say I didn't want anyone throwing cash at my clinic? How many?"

"Dusk."

"Get the hell out of my clinic."

"Are you kidding me?"

Dusk glared at him, darting forward to grab the coffee. "Taking this with me."

"*Dusk.*"

The raised eyebrow from Jesse when Dusk stormed into the clinic, shutting the door in Kent's face spoke volumes. The older man grabbed the extra cup of coffee. He waited while the younger man slammed around tiles of linoleum.

"Stupid move, Dr. Dusky."

"Oh?" He glanced over at Jesse with a tired grin. "How so?"

"Brings the expensive coffee, hires people to rebuild your baby, and you slam the door in his face? Stupidity at its finest." Jesse sat on one of the boxes of tiles. He blew on the coffee before taking a sip. "You realize it's not a weakness to ask for help."

"Don't need it."

"Dusk." Jesse placed his cup on the floor and leaned forward with his elbows on his knees. "I've been around a long time, kid. I've seen a lot of people who didn't deserve all the handouts they were given. You?

You deserve the help. Why the hell would you turn it away?"

"I—"

"Want to know what I think?" He wagged his finger at Dusk pointedly. "Good, I'm gonna tell you anyway. You got scared. You like him. He likes you. You got scared 'cause he ain't leaving town after a few days. You might end up more than liking him at some point, not now, or too soon, but in the future."

"Bullshit."

"Ain't bullshit if it's true." Jesse winked at him knowingly. He took a sip of his coffee and moved on to what was clearly the second part of his lecture. "You won't want anyone putting their money into the clinic. Ain't nothing wrong with being independent, Dusky. Why not tell the Mountain Man you want his manly hands to do the helping?"

"Could you make that sound dirtier?"

"Yep."

Dusk ran his fingers roughly through his hair, making it a shaggier mess than usual. "I did tell him."

"You threw a terrible-twos style tantrum, complete with slamming the door and stomping your feet."

"Fuck-a-doodle-do."

"Yep." Jesse held out an arm to stop him from running out of the clinic. "Give it a few days, Dusky.

How many times in January did you see the Mountain Man?"

"Dunno."

"Every day."

He reared his head back, instinctually trying to avoid the truth behind those two words. "Really?"

"So drink your coffee, let's finish this ugly ass floor, and then you can visit with him when you're thinking straight." Jesse pulled the lid off his cup. "Empty. *Shit.*"

Acknowledging the older man's wisdom, Dusk got to work on the linoleum. The drama from the morning motivated him to move faster than usual. They ended the day with most of the tiles laid out.

On the bike ride over to Kent's current project, Dusk cleared his mind. He could see what Jesse's point had been. It remained to be seen if his lover of the past three months would understand it.

Where the hell is his truck?

No truck, doors locked, no sign of him. Dusk tried giving him a call with no answer. He texted Derrick who mentioned seeing the Colorado-tagged vehicle heading toward the bridge leading out of the island.

Well, that's not good.

19

———

KENT

WHAT AM I DOING?

The three-hour drive to Miami hadn't cleared anything up in his mind. Kent sat in a parking space outside of his father's architecture firm, not certain why he'd made the trip in the first place. He couldn't recall ever fleeing to his step-father for advice on a moment of impulse.

Since when do I have moments of impulse? Oh, right, when I met the annoying, barefoot, dog walker. He dropped his head against the steering wheel with a groan. *I could've handled this all so much better.*

His mind kept drawing a blank on why Dusk had been so angry. Who refused help? Why wouldn't he at least attempt to talk it out with him?

Most of his previous relationships, even platonic friendships, had been with people who would call him out when he'd overstepped his boundaries. They tended to shove his face in it. Dusk had simply wanted him to leave.

"Kent?" Ramon knocked on the window. "What a wonderful surprise. I had no idea you would be heading up to see us so soon. Are you staying long?"

Kent lowered the driver-side window with his head still resting on the top of the steering wheel. "I thought we might have a late lunch?"

"Let me drive. I can listen while you share what's on your mind." Ramon stepped away from the truck. He glanced over his shoulder to a convertible Ford Mustang. "Casa Juancho has some of the best Spanish cuisine in Miami. Let me introduce you to the food of our family."

The ride over to the restaurant went silently for him wanting to talk to someone. His father took it in stride, likely happy simply to have more time together with him. Since they'd met at the end of last year, Kent had spoken with the man at least three times a week. Their tentative relationship continued to grow into a closer connection.

Over several courses of tapas and paella, Kent unloaded his quandary over Dusk on his father's shoulders. Ramon hadn't given him any sage advice. After sipping his wine, the man had suggested he respect the wishes of the person he wanted to help.

What?

"Did Dusk specifically say he preferred not to have others pay for the repairs to his clinic?" Ramon asked after a bite of his red wine poached pear.

"Several times."

"And so?"

"I—"

Ramon shook his fork at him, sending the thick reddish sauce flying. "As a young man, I tended to want to have complete control over everything in my life. I would often ignore the wishes of friends, family, even my beloved Caterina, believing I knew better."

"And did you?"

"Maybe." Ramon shrugged. "Not always, and certainly, being right never felt worth the effort of upsetting those I cared about."

"I wanted to be supportive."

"By throwing money at the problem?"

Hearing those words, ones Kent could recall using as an accusation toward his ex-husband, brought him up short. He had done what Spencer frequently did. *Damn it.* He should've known better.

"Why didn't he say something?" Kent thought

perhaps maybe he hadn't been listening enough. "He told me to leave."

"Kent? Son?" His father stretched his arm across the table to take his hand. "New romances always require negotiations and compromise. You've known each other for such a short time, your chemistry is undeniable. You can't expect to get everything right the first time. Talk to each other, give him some space to calm down, but talk to him. Does Dusk strike you as someone who enjoys conflict?"

"No."

The response sprang immediately to his mind. Dusk took mellow to a whole new level. He wouldn't have wanted to engage anyone in an argument, telling Kent to leave had likely been the extent of his showing aggravation.

Being a casual sexual relationship didn't mean Dusk didn't deserve his respect or consideration. The man had made his preferences crystal clear from the beginning. Hell, the educated veterinarian had been doing odd jobs for almost a year to earn enough funds to cover the repairs.

Deeper than his simply ignoring wishes, Kent had responded how he would've when married to Spencer. *Credit card, problem solved.* Dusk would've likely preferred him to bring his tools over. He'd said as much in fact, hadn't he?

God. Damn. It.

I should've listened.

20

DUSK

March

Two weeks had gone by since Dusk last saw Kent. He knew the exact number of days because every morning Jesse would mention it to him with a bemused grin. *Sadist.* Not even dumping a banana smoothie on his head had stopped the man.

He was a *very* dedicated sadist.

Progress on his clinic had continued; the flooring had gone in, been taken out when he screwed up, and redone the second time correctly. Dusk didn't care if anyone else understood why he wanted to do it all himself. He could look around the place and slowly return it to its former glory with an immense amount of pride.

I built this. I paid for it. I did this.

Drywall had gone into all of the rooms that had needed it. All the structural aspects of the rebuilding had been completed. Now he had to paint, lots of painting, and updating windows. It would be the final phase of the construction portion; after, would be all about making it his beautiful, homey clinic and getting it functional.

Busy days were the best. No time to think about missing Kent, or how ridiculous it was to miss him in the first place. No matter how often his dad, Jesse, and Derrick poked and prodded him on the subject until his mother had started swinging her rolling pin at them.

Love that woman.

A familiar truck sat in one of the parking spots across from his clinic. *What the hell?* Dusk cycled around to the back entrance, walking his bicycle inside to its usual resting spot behind the kennels. He strode through the surgery and receptionist areas to find Kent had laid out the tarps on the floor and already begun to put up painter's tape to protect the molding.

"Hey." Dusk stood stupidly in the middle of the room, watching the attractive older man. "What are you doing here?"

Kent's smile sent tingles down to the tips of his toes, which was annoying. He bent over to grab something hidden by the paint cans—his toolbox. "You said to bring my hammer."

"So I did." Dusk couldn't stop the smile from spreading across his face, so wide it hurt. "How's the house flipping?"

Kent crouched down to grab a screwdriver and opened the paint can Dusk set in front of him. "I spent a few weeks in Miami getting to know my father and his wife. It seemed more important than rushing through fixing up two houses. They're not going anywhere, the houses, I mean. I'll have plenty of time to work my magic. Thought maybe my hands would be welcome where my money wasn't."

"Kent…"

"No, you were right, I pushed, and I shouldn't have. I'm sorry." Kent stirred the paint slowly, though he seemed to watch Dusk out of the corner of his eye. "Want my help?"

"Apology accepted. Grab a brush." He decided not to draw out the apology. They'd both made mistakes. "How was Ramon?"

"Wise."

Dusk paused with a paint brush in hand, blue paint

dripping into the pan from the tip. "Is that good or bad?"

"Good." Kent laughed, sending another shiver through him. "He suggested I might want to get out of my own way, so I can enjoy myself."

"Definitely wise."

The first hour of painting had been awkward, conversation stilted while they walked on eggshells around each other. Dusk didn't want to prolong the angst from weeks ago, and Kent appeared intent on burying the hatchet. They both danced around each other, like their bodies were a mass of bruises they didn't want to risk brushing up against.

"We can't go on like this."

Dusk set the brush into the pan closest to him. "You're leaving?"

"What? No." Kent shook his head vehemently. His hand shot out like a bullet from a gun to catch Dusk by the neck. Strong fingers wrapped around the back of his neck to drag him over. His foot ended up in one of the pans of paint, something he failed to notice when those lips he'd missed closed over his. He pulled back to breathe after a moment. "Damn, I missed this."

They kissed. *And kissed.* Clothes had started to come off when applause sounded from near the front of the clinic. Dusk peered around Kent to find an amused audience of two watching.

"Oh, thank God. Now you'll stop moping around like I stole your bicycle." Derrick winked at them before backing out of the room, leaving Jesse by the front door. "Your mother says to come by for lunch in an hour."

Jesse's eyes drifted down their bodies to where the two men's shoes had stepped in and out of the paint. "Might want to clean up a bit. Hand print on the ass won't win you any points with the parents."

"*Jesse.*"

"See you at the bar, Dr. Dusky." Jesse turned his attention to Kent. "Remember what I said, Mountain Man."

Dusk watched him leave with a confused frown. "What did he tell you?"

"Nothing important." Kent eased himself out of the puddle of paint on the tarp. "Think we got more paint on the floor than on the wall."

"We can fix it." Dusk couldn't keep his eyes away from the man, wondering if this might be about more than fixing his little animal hospital.

While Kent had been in Miami, Dusk had spent time talking with Derrick who had asked him what he wanted out of a relationship. *Not marriage.* He'd enjoyed what had started to develop with Kent. What could be more perfect than dating, sex, laughing together? It didn't need to be more complicated.

"So, you sticking around for lunch?" Dusk nudged the man with his foot.

"Definitely."

"More than lunch?"

"*Definitely.*" Kent slid a hand into one of Dusk's front pockets, fingers straying along his thigh. "Have you got space in your life for a man from the mountains?"

"For now. I can always have Jesse make you disappear." Dusk laughed until Kent shoved him up against the freshly painted wall. "We're making a mess."

"Don't care. I'll be here to help you clean it up."

"Yes, you will."

ARE YOU READY TO FALL OFF THE pitch and into love? You can do so in my international bestselling gay romance series, The Sin Bin. Each book features hot rugby players and the men who steal their hearts.

Start the series today with **The Wanderer.**

Needing more sweetness, hilarious antics, and a stand-alone? Why not check out **Pure Dumb Luck**? When two small-town country dudes win the lottery, they finally find the courage to speak their truth. An unexpected adventure follows.

ALSO BY DAHLIA DONOVAN

THE GRASMERE COTTAGE MYSTERY TRILOGY

Dead in the Garden - Dead in the Pond - Dead in the Shop

MOTTS COLD CASE MYSTERY SERIES

Poisoned Primrose

Pierced Peony

LONDON PODCAST MYSTERY SERIES

Cosplay Killer

STAND-ALONE ROMANCES

After the Scrum

At War With A Broken Heart

Forged in Flood

Found You

One Last Heist

Pure Dumb Luck

Here Comes The Son

All Lathered Up

Not Even A Mouse

The Misguided Confession

THE SIN BIN (COMPLETE SERIES)

The Wanderer - The Caretaker - The Royal Marine -

The Botanist - The Unexpected Santa

The Lion Tamer - Haka Ever After

ABOUT THE AUTHOR

Dahlia Donovan wrote her first romance series after a crazy dream about shifters and damsels in distress. She prefers irreverent humour and unconventional characters. An autistic and occasional hermit, her life wouldn't be complete without her husband and her massive collection of books and video games.

Join Dahlia's newsletter:
http://eepurl.com/Q0n0X

Dahlia would love to hear from you directly, too. Please feel free to email her at dahlia@dahliadonovan.com or check out her website dahliadonovan.com for updates.

facebook.com/dahliadonovan
twitter.com/DahliaDonovan
instagram.com/dahliadonovanauthor
bookbub.com/authors/dahlia-donovan

ACKNOWLEDGMENTS

Thanks must go out to my betas and all the amazing people at Hot Tree Publishing—Becky, the editors, cover designer, etc., who get me through the writing process with my mind mostly intact.

Also, to my husband for having the patience of a saint--thank you for always supporting me.

And lastly, a massive thank you to Renee for the chickens. Brilliant. Completely. Brilliant.

ABOUT THE PUBLISHER

Hot Tree Publishing opened its doors in 2015 with an aspiration to bring quality fiction to the world of readers. With the initial focus on romance and a wide spread of romance subgenres, Hot Tree Publishing has since opened their first imprint, Tangled Tree Publishing, specializing in crime, mystery, suspense, and thriller.

Firmly seated in the industry as a leading editing provider to independent authors and small publishing houses, Hot Tree Publishing is the sister company to Hot Tree Editing, founded in 2012. Having established in-house editing and promotions, plus having a well-respected market presence, Hot Tree Publishing endeavors to be a leader in bringing quality stories to the world of readers.

Interested in discovering more amazing reads brought to you by Hot Tree Publishing? Head over to the website for information:

www.hottreepublishing.com

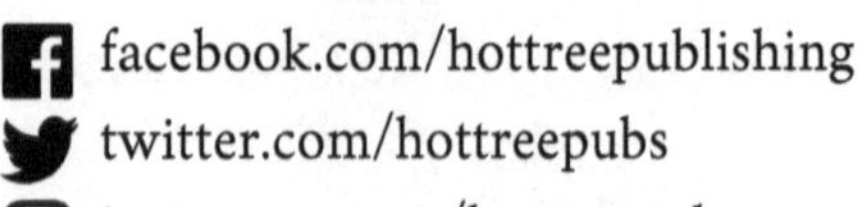

facebook.com/hottreepublishing
twitter.com/hottreepubs
instagram.com/hottreepubs